Tadpoles

Joshua Britton

Bird Brain Publishing

To Delight, Instruct, and Inspire
Evansville, Indiana

Tadpoles by Joshua Britton
Cover Art: Frank Gordon
Graphic Design: Whitney Arvin
Author Photo: Amber Heerdink
ISBN 978-1-937668-04-4
Bird Brain Publishing
www.birdbrainpublishing.com

Summary: Twelve tales of children struggling with childhood and parents grappling with parenthood, told with wit and sympathy.

For Z and T

CONTENTS

"Never grow up... always down."

Roald Dahl

"Anybody who has survived his childhood has enough information about life to last him the rest of his days."

Flannery O'Connor

"Grown up, and that is a terribly hard thing to do. It is much easier to skip it and go from one childhood to another."

F. Scott Fitzgerald

"Adults are just obsolete children and to hell with them."

Dr. Seuss

TADPOLES

THE FIRST TIME I WENT CAMPING, I hopped some rocks to cross a shallow creek flowing down the mountain so my feet wouldn't get wet. It warmed my father's heart to see me doing that. He said he was sorry I wasn't growing up in the country.

Greg lived across the street from me. I didn't have a television, but he did. I didn't think I was missing anything, though, until I went to school and us kids got old enough to have actual conversations. When the conversation got around to last night's episodes, I usually got quiet.

Sometimes I watched Greg's television. He was pretty cool, a year older than me, and I liked going over to his house. Usually, though, unless it was storming outside, we got kicked out of the house after a little. Greg's mom said sitting in front of a television was no way to spend a beautiful day.

There were woods out back. They weren't big woods. From Greg's backyard we could walk through the woods and end up in someone else's backyard in less than ten minutes. But it seemed enormous. Greg called the woods a "forest" in front of his father once, and his father laughed at him. Greg never said "forest" again.

We built a fort out of dead branches and rotting logs. We worked on it long and hard before we finished a four-sided hut that was plenty comfortable as long as nobody stood up. We laid a bunch of sticks across the top for a roof and filled in the cracks with as many twigs as would stay up.

Both Greg and I came from homes with basements, so the next step was to dig a basement for the fort. It was tough, carrying the dirt and clay through the door without knocking the walls down with either end of the shovel, but it only fell down twice.

Greg complained about the growing dirt mound outside our fort. He said it would upset the neighbors. I looked around but didn't see any neighbors. I suggested we put the dirt up top to fill in the cracks so inside we could have total shade.

"That's a good idea," Greg said. "You do that. I'm gonna keep digging."

I piled mud on top with my bare hands and filled in every crack. I smoothed the mud out with the palm of my hand, and it looked good. I felt like a pioneer man. I was proud of myself.

I took a ten-second walk to the creek to rinse the dirt off my hands. It wasn't really a creek, just a concrete drainage gutter that cut through the woods that couldn't have been more perfectly placed.

Sometimes, after it rained, it flowed pretty hard, but usually it was no more than six inches wide, and half an inch deep. If there couldn't be a real creek, the next best thing was a fake one put in by the town.

I felt raindrops as I was scrubbing my hands. I ran back to the fort to tell Greg, who was still shoveling away inside. He was all set to run home, but I pointed out that we could wait out the rain in our fort because of the roof I'd just packed down. So we stayed.

It rained harder, and the wind picked up. I started getting nervous our fort was going to tip over. Everything was going okay, though, until some of the roof fell onto my lap. I wiped it off before Greg could see, but it left a mud stain on my shorts. Then more pieces of mud started falling, and some landed in Greg's hair.

"Your roof is garbage!" he said.

He got out and ran home through the rain. I followed.

After it stopped raining, we went back, afraid of what we might find. The walls were still upright, but the roof didn't look functional. All of the dirt, mud, and clay had fallen inside, and a lot of the twigs were in there, too.

"This is stupid," Greg said. "I'll be right back."

I started picking the twigs out of the mud while waiting for Greg to come back. I put the twigs next to the remains of the dirt pile outside.

Greg came back with a blue tarp that he took from his garage. He said at least this way the roof wouldn't fall apart again. I helped put it in place. Greg called it the "new and improved roof."

SOMETIMES GREG WAS A ZOMBIE when watching TV. There were a couple of shows I liked, but if they weren't on, I started spending time outside by myself. I stood next to our little concrete creek, wishing it were bigger. I lost my balance and my foot landed in the water. The water was so shallow, though, that it didn't go higher than the sole of my sneaker, and the water didn't even seep through to my foot. I wished it were deeper. I grabbed the shovel from inside our fort, took a pile of dirt, and dumped it in the water. The water backed up a bit and got deeper before trickling around the dirt. My dam gradually eroded away and within minutes it was as if there hadn't been anything there at all.

I tried again. This time I dropped in rocks. I dropped in sticks and twigs to fill in the cracks and dumped a whole mess of leaves and dirt in to seal it off. Soon the water was even deeper than the first time. Some water still seeped through cracks, but it seemed sturdy enough. I was proud of myself. I ran to tell Greg what I had made. He thought it was cool.

IN GENERAL, WHEN GREG WAS THERE, I didn't get much time with the shovel. Practically all he wanted to do was dig. His new plan was to dig a tunnel from outside the fort to the inside. He said this way it would be easier to escape our enemies.

"Who's our enemies?" I asked.

"Anyone not on our side."

"No one's on our side," I said. "Except us."

He nodded gravely. I got goosebumps and my heartbeat faster. I looked around for logs and branches to build my own fort. The one we had was getting too intense.

One day Greg came over to my house and told me that he had fixed my dam. I didn't know there had been anything wrong with my dam, but Greg wouldn't tell me anything; he was so adamant that I see it for myself.

The rocks, sticks, leaves and mud from my dam had been kicked out of the way. Greg made his own dam using an old car tire and some bricks he found lying around in his garage. He was awfully proud.

"This is better," he insisted. "The other one looked like it was going to fall apart any second.

The water was about as deep as before. Except for the blue tarp, the tire seemed out of place in the woods, but it got the job done.

MY NEW FORT WASN'T VERY GOOD. Most of the good pieces of wood had been used on what became Greg's fort. And he kept adding on, trying to turn it into a castle. My fort had only three walls, and the roof only went halfway across. Greg started calling me neighbor.

THE CREEK WAS DEEP ENOUGH that it made a nice wash basin. I liked going down there to rinse the dirt off my hands, even though they'd be covered again in two seconds. But one time, when I knelt down to dip in my hands, I stopped. The water looked wrong. The bottom was lined with something I had never seen before. It looked like slime. Or maybe pollution. Pollution was all my second-grade teacher had seemed to want to talk about.

I ran back to tell Greg. He raced to the creek, and laughed when he saw.

"Those are frog eggs!" he said.

"How do you know?" I asked.

"I saw it on TV."

I beamed. I couldn't believe I was creating life. Greg said I didn't do anything, that the frogs had done all the work, and that, if anything, it was his tire that did the work. I was still proud.

After that, there was nothing I wanted more than to see those eggs hatch. Nothing else mattered. I had seen frogs in pet stores, or in the bushes, or occasionally hopping through the lawn. I had never seen a tadpole. They seemed weird. How can you be a tadpole and a frog in the same life? How come butterflies are caterpillars first? I wished I could turn into something different, like maybe a cheetah.

All Greg could think about now was a new business venture. Once the tadpoles turned into frogs, he was going to sell them to pet stores and get rich. I said I didn't want to kidnap frogs to sell to people. He told me that if we didn't, most of them would probably either starve or get eaten by birds. I asked how much money we were going to get.

Greg's father took back the tarp from the original fort, but Greg didn't even care. Mostly he thought about the future. He made a list of pet stores we were going to visit once the frogs were hatched. He dreamed about all the money we were going to make. Half the time he thought he might invest the money into more animals and start his own pet store. The rest of the time he talked about what he was going to spend it on. He considered everything, from a box-full of Snickers bars, to a new car, to moving out of his parents' house.

I checked on the eggs five times a day. I was so afraid they were going to hatch when I wasn't around. I couldn't wait. I wanted to tell everyone I knew, but Greg made me promise not to tell a soul. He didn't want anyone to steal our idea, so I kept my mouth shut. We were going to make so much money. Greg said I could have a hundred dollars once he sold them all. That was more money than I'd ever seen.

———

GREG WAS WATCHING A CARTOON with robots and lasers, so I went to the woods by myself. It had rained most of the previous day and there were a lot of puddles I tried and failed to avoid.

The creek was black. I couldn't see the bottom. The water was busy, like it was boiling. There were hundreds of them! There were thousands! I was so excited. I wanted to stick my hands in and pick some up, but I didn't want them to eat my skin off. How long had I waited? Days? Weeks? They had finally hatched. Millions of tadpoles were swimming around, bumping into each other head first, trying to get somewhere, with nowhere to go. Soon there would be millions of frogs jumping through our neighborhood, and Greg and I would have our hands full chasing them down.

I ran as fast as I could to give Greg the news, tripping and falling only a couple of times. I was out of breath when I got to his living room, where he was still lying on the couch, watching TV. He quickly put on some shoes and raced ahead of me to the creek.

"We're gonna be rich!" I heard him yell while I struggled to catch up.

Then he ran back home and said to follow him. He rummaged through his garage and pulled out four buckets. I didn't know what they were for until he said it would be easier to catch tadpoles than it would be to catch frogs. He was so smart.

Back at the creek, Greg bent down and

scooped up a bucketful of water. I looked inside and it was filled to the brim with tadpoles colliding with each other. He filled another bucket up and told me to do the same. My bucket I could only fill halfway, though, so he did the last one himself.

"It's too dangerous to leave them out here in the wild," Greg said. "We have to put them in your garage. That way they'll be protected."

"Why can't they go in yours?" I said.

"My dad wouldn't like it."

I didn't know where to put them, but Greg said they would be fine on the floor. So we put them between the wall and the minivan.

"Lemme know when they turn into frogs," he said. "Then we'll sell them and get rich."

"You said you're gonna give me a hundred dollars," I reminded him.

"I know," he said. "We're gonna be set for life."

Greg went home and I was left with the tadpoles. They were a lot smaller than I thought they would be.

I got afraid of what my mom would say. Frogs eat bugs. My mom might say without all the frogs to eat them there would be tons of bees and mosquitoes, and we could never go outside. I couldn't let her know I had them.

There was a shelf high up on the wall of the

garage mostly empty except for motor oil, air filters, and a paint can. I didn't think my mom would see the buckets if I put them up there. I got a ladder and climbed with the first bucket. It was only noticeable if you specifically looked up. I carried the next one up, and then another. With the buckets so high I wouldn't be able to follow the progress of their transformation, but, looking around the garage, it still seemed like the best plan. I put the last bucket on the shelf. The shelf cracked in half.

I fell backward off the ladder and hit my head on the floor of the garage. When I came to, and after I felt the bump on the back of my head, I looked around and saw the garage floor flooded with water and tadpoles sputtering about. I panicked. The dream was in trouble. I tried to pick one up but I couldn't get a grip. They were making it so difficult I couldn't even get one off the ground.

I needed a faster way to get a whole bunch of tadpoles into the bucket at one time. I ran into the house to grab a broom and dustpan. I dropped the dustpan and began to sweep the tadpoles into it. It didn't work. The broom smeared the tadpoles into a paste against the concrete floor. I had killed dozens before even realizing it. I gave up and stepped back to think of another plan, simultaneously squashing a few more with my shoes. They were everywhere, and they were slowing down.

They needed more water. I pivoted quickly to

get the hose but I slipped in a puddle. I ended up on my back. When I turned my head, there were tadpoles inches from my face. I turned my head the other way and saw more of the same. I stood up and stepped on a few, and saw some more crushed where I had been lying. My back was wet, and it probably had bodies on it, too. The water was thinning throughout the garage, and many of the tadpoles had stopped moving. There was nothing I could do. It was over.

Greg's wrath was going to be the end of me. If he didn't kill me, my father's disappointment would. I took one last look at the carnage on the concrete floor before I walked across the street with my head down. Let's get it over with, I thought.

UNEARTHING

WHEN HE LEANS BACK to catch his breath from retching, Tom's elbows dig into the grass. Across the yard is the hole. Once he catches his breath he'll crawl back over and look down again.

This isn't Tom's backyard, it's Amber's. She's been openly jealous of her neighbors' landscaping skills. But Amber's front yard is small and has a gigantic century-old tree smack-dab in the middle, and its fat protruding roots make it difficult to plant grass, let alone a few bushes. There is an equally large deciduous tree behind the house, but the backyard is bigger. Tom had selected a patch of lawn far enough away from the tree where he figured three equidistant holes could be dug for three identical bushes that, once grown in, would not only be a cosmetic improvement but would also obscure the rotting fence dividing Amber's yard from her neighbor's.

But, while digging his first hole, Tom struck something hard. He assumed it was just a rogue, water-seeking root, and he hacked away.

Now he reaches into the hole, picks out a

clump of clay, and brushes off dirt to confirm what he thought he saw before: a human head.

More gagging. More dry heaves. Until now his biggest worry was how to tell his parents he's gotten his girlfriend pregnant.

"There's a dead body in the backyard!" Tom says into the phone. "I was doing yard work and I dug it up! You need to send someone over quick!"

9-1-1 asks follow-up questions, and he answers: "I found it just now." "I think a man, not sure." "About two feet deep." "Months. Maybe years, I don't know!" "No, I don't recognize him!" "With a shovel. I might've damaged it. Like, cut it." "Please hurry!" "What do you mean you'll try?! Somebody is dead! Please get over here as soon as possible!" "Tomorrow?! What are you talking about? Today! Someone needs to come over today!"

"You haven't turned on a television recently, sir, have you?" the operator says.

"No. Why?"

"There's been a school shooting today. All of our officers are at the site."

"Oh no," – Amber is a high school teacher! – "which school?"

"Central." A momentary sigh of relief; Amber teaches at North. "Turn on the TV, sir, and we'll get an officer out to you when we can."

Tom obeys. All of the news channels are

covering the Central shooting. So far, three students and a teacher are known to be dead. The authorities assume more, though they haven't yet entered the building; they think the shooters are still inside. Dozens of students are unaccounted for, but whether they're dead, they've become hostages, or they've simply run off without telling anyone is unknown.

Tom looks out the window. He'd spent several hours online, and several more at Home Depot, to settle on three self-sufficient arborvitaes that wouldn't die when he and Amber inevitably forget to take care of them. His landscaping project, which *seemed* like a great idea, probably isn't going to happen now, even after the excavation.

Back at his hole, and the modest dirt pile next to it, he covers his mouth at the sight of the head, but he's gained more control of his gag reflex in the last few minutes. The shrubs lean against the fence. His shovel lays flat on the ground. As unappetizing an idea as it may be, the more of the body he exposes now, the quicker it will be gone once the proper authorities arrive. He won't try to remove it, only to uncover the rest. He picks up his shovel.

"What are you doing?!"

"Amber, don't come over here!" Tom says. He drops his shovel and rushes to her side. "There's a dead body buried there."

"No, I mean, why are you digging?"

"I was going to plant those for you," he says,

pointing at the potted arborvitaes. "As a surprise. But there's a dead person, Amber. A man, I think. The police should be here soon. I just called them."

"You did what?!"

Amber turns around and rushes into the house. Tom quickly follows. He'd left the TV on and he glances at footage of police and SWAT ready to bust into the school.

"Where are you going?" Tom calls after her. She's not that concerned about the body, he thinks. "Why are you home so early?"

"All the schools shut down because of the shooting," she says. She tosses clothes into a suitcase she's pulled out of the closet. "You called the police, you say?"

"Yes, but they're busy at Central."

"Still," she says, "they know." She zips up her suitcase and stands it upright. "Do you have any cash?"

Tom nods toward his wallet on the bed stand. He has a lot of cash, Amber is pleased to discover, and she takes it all.

"I need to leave," she says. Tom is speechless. She kisses him. "I'm so sorry."

– They know what?!

WHEN TOM WAS A TEENAGER, he figured out that his oldest uncle was born only four months after his grandparents got married. He confronted his mother about this startling revelation, but she excused his grandparents by saying, "They loved each other a little too much."

– Mom, Dad, I'm going to be a father.

– Oh, well, Son, that's okay; these things happen. So when do I get to meet my future daughter-in-law?

For weeks Tom has been thinking of little else. He should be grateful for so big a distraction.

When Amber told him they were pregnant, she listed abortion among their options. Tom was conflicted. He was against abortion, at least that's what his church always taught. On the other hand, how much simpler life would be right now if there wasn't a baby on its way. Turned out, he didn't have a say; Amber was humoring him and had already decided to keep it.

"Let's get married!" Tom said. Just because the baby was conceived illegitimately doesn't mean it has to be born illegitimately. And besides, he thought he wanted to marry her anyway.

"You're sweet, but no."

"You don't want to marry me?"

"Maybe. But if I do, it won't be because of this."

Tom's grandparents married before they turned twenty. His parents married during college. Tom is the middle child of seven, the only one not yet hitched, and the only one without children of his own. He'd let all this slip early on, and Amber correctly inferred that her new boyfriend was desperate for a wife. She'd had no intention of *re*-marrying, or at least not so soon. When she did involuntarily imagine happily growing old with Tom, she got annoyed with herself. To stave off his pressuring, she turned the tables and pressured him into bed. Tom had been committed to preserving his virginity until marriage, but she wore him down. Amber knew that in Tom's eyes sex was one of the major perks of marriage, and now he had it without the legal commitment. Now all talks of marriage could be shelved. It worked remarkably well, until it backfired.

Seventeen confirmed dead: two teachers and fifteen students. This isn't the worst school shooting of all time, but it's up there. The school has been searched once and is being searched again, but most everyone has accepted that somehow the killers, now identified as high school freshmen, have gotten away. With the suspects at large, nobody will sleep well tonight. Over a thousand students and two hundred employees, the police can't possibly protect everyone.

The networks broadcast pictures of the deceased. Tom doesn't recognize any of them. Amber works at a different school, but he wonders anyway if she knew either of the murdered teachers. Overall, though, his mind is elsewhere, and he watches the coverage with less horror than he did past mass shootings.

Where is she? he wonders. Where did she take our baby? What happened to the guy in the backyard? Sooner or later, he'll have to explain to his parents that not only has he gotten his girlfriend pregnant – a girlfriend they haven't even met yet! – but that the baby will almost definitely be born a bastard. Suddenly, that doesn't seem so bad compared to this new scenario:

– Mom, Dad, your next grandchild will be born in prison...

"I made a mistake!" he blurts. "It's not a human body. It's a dog. I didn't look very closely and I overreacted. But I've double checked, and it's definitely a dog. The police don't need to come anymore."

"Okay, sir. Noted."

– My girlfriend's dog died a couple of years ago. This was before we started going out. She told me once it was buried in the backyard, but I forgot.

That's believable, Tom convinces himself. That's what I'll say if they follow up.

He makes another call, but Amber's cell vibrates on the end table next to him. Tom hits "end", frustrated that she left her phone behind.

In the backyard, Tom takes another look inside his hole. He's been to funerals, but this is the least healthy corpse he's ever seen. He takes his shovel and dumps in enough dirt to re-cover the body. For the next step, Tom waits for dark.

OUT OF RESPECT FOR THE VICTIMS of the Central High School shooting, a moment of silence precedes the baseball game. Tom watches from the comfort of his home. Well, Amber's home. Tom still has his apartment, though he's been spending far more than half his time here, another secret he's kept from his parents.

– I'm almost thirty years old, Mom! I'm flesh and blood. What do you expect from me? How many more failed engagements do I need to go through?

When the time comes, hopefully Tom will maintain composure better in real life than he does in his imagination.

The networks have shown nothing but coverage of the shooting, even now, during primetime hours. The manhunt continues, and Tom flips between the news reports and the ballgame.

Another catcher's visit to the mound, another pickoff throw to first base, another excruciating seven-pitch walk, the innings crawl by slowly. He wants this episode of his life to be over, but the game is only halfway through, and outside it's only dusk.

"You must be Tom."

Tom jumps up from the couch, startled. Who just walks in uninvited?

"Who are you? Are you a cop? What are you doing here?"

"You've got guilty written all over you," the intruder says. He walks through the house and out the backdoor, surveys the situation, and comes back inside. "I'm assuming no one's been here yet?"

"Everyone's busy with the shooting," Tom says. "Who are you?"

"Did they give an ETA by any chance?"

Tom doesn't respond.

"Relax, Tom, God. I'm not real thrilled with you digging up the past, but I'm here to help." Tom feels the urge to wet himself. Sensing his nerves, the visitor offers a handshake. "Derrick, all right? Amber asked me to check things out." Rather than shake the hand, Tom crosses his legs. Derrick gestures toward the bathroom, says, "Go ahead," and Tom scampers off.

By the time Tom finishes relieving himself, Derrick has opened one of Amber's beers and has taken Tom's spot on the couch. Amber has an ex named Derrick, Tom remembers, though how long ago and to what degree of significance, he's not sure.

"How do you know Amber?"

"I haven't seen her in a couple of years, actually," Derrick says. "Have barely even heard from her, in fact. You see someone every day for a year, and then not at all – it's an interesting phenomenon."

Tom lets this sink in. "Every day?"

"Husbands and wives tend to live together, Tom."

All Tom knows is that he doesn't know anything. He's been in denial about the possibility she might've slept with someone before him. But now, in addition to having impregnated a fugitive out of wedlock who doesn't want to get married, she's a divorcée. His parents are going to throw a fit.

"No one's coming," Tom says. "I called back and said I made a mistake. I said it's a dog."

"Good thinking," Derrick says. "Relax, man." He pats the couch cushion next to him and again offers to shake Tom's hand. "We've got a long night ahead of us. Do you want a beer?"

Tom gives in, sits down, and shakes Derrick's hand. "I don't drink," he says.

THE FLASHING LIGHTS ARE BLINDING. Tom has gone through a stop like this before. They'd surrounded a couple of bars and were checking for DUI. "I've never drank in my life," he told the uniforms, amused, even proud of himself. But that was years ago, and he can't honestly say that anymore, though he's still never been drunk. This time, however, alcohol isn't the issue, and now he's nervous.

"I've never touched a dead body in my life!" The windows are closed, and he screams inside the car. "It wasn't me!"

— I got my girlfriend pregnant, though. We loved each other a little too much.

At least the arborvitaes are planted. "Amber told me about your idea," Derrick had said. "It's cute. First thing tomorrow morning, though, you're going to want to scour the yard and make sure we didn't miss anything." Two were planted into either end of the expanded and human-sized hole, and a separate hole was dug for the third. They're not symmetrically spaced apart as Tom had planned, but it'll do.

The body didn't lift out in one piece, and Tom threw up, this time for real. What a nightmare, though Derrick didn't seem to be having much fun either.

With its loose limbs folded tightly in a tarp, the body was dropped into the trunk of *his* car, not Derrick's; Tom wasn't given a choice. He's been following Derrick, but Derrick has made it to the other side, and Tom has nowhere to go.

As if the strobing lights on top of the police cars aren't bad enough, a flashlight blasts into his face.

"Have you seen either of these kids?"

The flashlight shines onto the photographs. Tom looks and recognizes the kids as the shooters. "Just on the news," he says. "They're still out there?"

The cop nods and waves Tom along.

Tom exhales and puts the car in drive. The car stalls, and the cop looks annoyed. Tom's face burns. He restarts the engine and pulls through.

Derrick leads him to a secluded farmhouse. Already dug and waiting for them is a hole, behind the barn and next to a woodpile. The two men lift the body out of Tom's trunk and dump it in the hole. Derrick grabs hold of the tarp and yanks it free, like pulling a table cloth out from under dishes. He soaks the remains with lighter fluid and then tosses in a lit lighter. With the body aflame, Derrick throws logs from the woodpile on top.

He takes out his phone. "I think we're good." He listens for a moment. "Sure." He hangs up.

"Was that Amber?" Tom asks.

Derrick nods and gives him permission to leave. "Until next time, Tom," he says.

Derrick doesn't offer to shake hands, nor does Tom say goodbye. He's thrilled to distance himself from Derrick and the farmhouse. He's hurt that Amber didn't ask to talk to him. He doesn't know how to reach her, and he wonders if he'll ever see her again, but then an unfamiliar number flashes on his cell phone screen.

"Derrick says we're in the clear," Amber says.

"Apparently," Tom says. "We."

"I'm sorry about all this."

"It happens." Tom rolls his eyes at himself, and he's angry at the woman he's hoping to bind himself to forever. "Who was that?"

"Derrick or the other guy?"

"The other guy."

"Do you really want to know?"

He guesses not. "Was he a bad guy, at least?"

"The worst."

Tom has a burning desire never to talk about this again.

"Where are you?" he asks.

"In an uncomfortable motel room without a car. Will you come pick me up?"

WHEN TOM PULLS INTO THE PARKING LOT, his headlights blind two bums leaning against the side of a dumpster. "Sorry," he says. He's recently been blinded by a police flashlight, so he knows it's not much fun.

Amber steps out of her motel room into the chilly pre-dawn air and wraps her arms around Tom's middle.

"Thanks for coming," she says, her suitcase at her side.

"Do you want to meet my parents this weekend?"

"Okay," she says. "And you need to meet mine.

Maybe we can talk about planning for a wedding."

"Really?!" Suddenly this has become one of Tom's better days.

Amber likes Tom, there's no denying. Derrick had been a mistake; he'd admit it himself. She agreed to go out with Tom because he was safe. But Tom's not only a nice guy who treats her well; she's grown to love him. She's not any good at being a rebel, and today he's really come through. As much as she tried to fight it, the pregnancy made marriage seem inevitable. But now, why prolong the inevitable?

Tomorrow is going to be a good day, Tom thinks. He'll call in sick. All the schools are closed for the rest of the week, so Amber won't work either. They'll sleep in and have breakfast in their underwear. He'll call his parents, the first step toward telling them about the baby. Maybe he'll call his siblings, too, and invite them all to dinner. It'll be like a family reunion! They might all gang up on him, but at least at the end of the evening he'll be able to walk out with Amber.

Tom smiles all the way to Amber's house. They hold hands, which rest on her lap next to her belly. Sometimes, when she doesn't have a shirt on, Tom thinks he can see the beginning of a baby bump.

Tom doesn't know everything, he's aware. Nobody has told him how the body came to be buried in her backyard, or, as between Amber and Derrick, who the biggest culprit was. He doesn't *want* to know. He could dig deeper and try to unearth Amber's past, but people who don't know anything are generally happier.

"This is really nice," Amber says, as Tom shows her the upgraded backyard. They are home and the sun is on its way up. "Thank you."

"Your motel room was number 115, right?" Tom asks.

Amber nods. After she'd vacated the hotel, Tom offered the room to the two bums he'd seen at the edge of the parking lot. Tom is such a charitable guy that, even though Amber worries that the bums will trash the place and she'll get blamed, it's hard not to admire his devotion to mankind.

Tom pulls out his cell phone and dials three digits.

"Hi, yes, you know the kids from the school shooting? I think they're in a motel room. Let me give you the address."

THE DOG'S FAULT

DAD SHOULD STAY. He's here every day anyway, straight from work, still wearing a suit and tie except on casual Fridays. Mom serves baked ziti for dinner and dad sits across from Davina and me, like we're still a family. What's the point of his apartment? Is it so terrible sleeping in the same house as the rest of us?

Mom used to stand on her tip-toes to kiss dad goodbye every morning before he left for work. I don't remember when that stopped. Maybe after we got Harold. Harold is hairy and beautiful, but also loud and badly-behaved. He stole pizza off dad's plate. Dad has never liked Harold. He prefers cats, but mom and Davina are allergic.

Teenagers have all the freedom. Davina has a job and a driver's license. Half the time she doesn't eat dinner with us, and she stays out past eleven. She feels bad for me, "little Danny," because I get carted around by our parents.

Dinners without her aren't so bad, though. I like Davina, but I get more attention without her.

Harold lingers under the table, suckering handouts from mom and me, and dad only occasionally complains about him. Then dad whisks me away while mom does the dishes.

I'd like to bring Harold, but I don't even ask. Harold goes ape every time dad comes over, as if he doesn't remember that he and dad lived together for a couple of months. Dad takes it personally, but he shouldn't; Harold attacks whomever comes through the door. Except mom. He takes care of mom. He sleeps on mom's bed.

My neighborhood has a lot of kids. The conservative Italian Catholics go to religion class every day after private school, while the indifferent Italian Catholics are more available. The agnostics' dad casually swears in front of me, and I'm pretty sure the Unitarians' parents smoke Mary Jane. The Methodist children are all adopted. I'm unique, it turns out. Everybody's parents live together except mine.

"Hey Danny," Joel says. "What's wrong?"

"My parents are separating," I confide in him.

Joel doesn't go to church. He lives in a different neighborhood and we ride the bus together. I can ride my bike to his house in ten minutes. I have to be careful, though. His neighborhood isn't as nice as mine. The trees hang over the road and there's garbage in the gutters. Nobody's parents are married in Joel's neighborhood, not even Joel's.

"That stinks. Divorce stinks."

"They're not getting divorced," I clarify. "Just separated."

"What's the difference?"

"They might get married again."

"You think that'll happen?"

"I don't know. How long were *your* parents separated before they got divorced?"

"My parents were never married."

Mom cooks ziti and tortellini, like we're Italian, even though we're not. Joel's not Italian, either, but most people are. There's a fat kid named Leone on our baseball team. He always bats last, but by rule he has to play the field for at least four innings. Destino has a stranglehold on center field, but with Leone out there, Destino shades pretty far toward right to help cover his ground. Joel is good, but Destino is the second coming of DiMaggio, according to Moretti, our catcher. After victories, we get free pizza at Pontillo's, our team sponsor, because our second baseman's grandfather is the owner, except his mom's name changed to Gruttadauria when she got married.

At third base I see dad arrive. He misses the first inning or two because of work, but he wears a hat and brings a glove so we can play catch between innings. He cheers, "Yay Danny!" when I get a hit. Then, he sits next to mom; she brings an extra folding chair for him. Davina never comes to my games, so with dad, mom has someone to keep her company.

———

AT FIRST I'M ONLY CONFUSED.

Dad sits me down in the family room, just the two of us in the entire house. This is when he tells me they're splitting up.

"Is it because of Harold?" I ask. I look around the room, but I don't see him. My throat is tight, like I'm choking, and my eyes are blurry and wet.

"No, Danny, it's not because of Harold."

"But you don't like Harold."

"Harold has nothing to do with it."

"Then why?"

He frowns. "Your mother and I aren't happy anymore."

I'm not getting the full story, I realize, and I might ask "why" for the rest of my life. If Harold isn't a factor, whose fault is it? Eventually I suggest we throw the ball around in the backyard, to dad's relief. I ask him to get into a catcher's crouch. Hard and on point, I fire away, hitting all my spots, the best I've ever pitched.

I NEVER GET THE FULL STORY WITH ANYTHING. Like when Davina ran away. She was gone over twenty-four hours before my parents tracked her down, hiding out with a friend my parents didn't know. She was drunk, too. And no one even told me she'd been gone until long after it was over. Mom mentioned it casually one time, like it wasn't a big deal.

"Are you going to come to dad's tonight?" I ask Davina. I go almost every night, and while it's nice having dad to myself, sometimes I wish she'd come too.

"Yeah right," she says, rolling her eyes.

Davina hasn't come to dad's with me in weeks, maybe months. When she does come, she mostly talks to her friends on the phone in a different room. Dad says it's okay; that's just what teenage girls do. But she doesn't talk on the phone this much when we're at mom's.

"Why does Davina hate dad so much?" I ask mom.

"She's having a hard time forgiving him," mom says. "And that's my fault. Your father didn't like the reason I gave Davina for dad moving out. So dad decided he'd be the one to tell you, by himself, so it would go over better."

"What *was* the reason?" I ask.

She kisses me on the head, and I know she won't tell me.

I think Davina needs to get over it. The separation is the same no matter how we were told. And besides, barely anything has changed. Like how dad comes over for dinner all the time. And he's coming on Christmas morning, too. He doesn't come to the Christmas Eve service at church, though.

"I wanted dad to see me be a wise man," I complain.

"Dad isn't allowed to come to church with us anymore," mom says.

"Everyone can come to church."

"Not dad. The elders told him not to even step foot inside."

"What? Why?"

"Oh, never mind."

Kicked out of church? When did that happen? And for what? There are other divorced people in our church, I'm pretty sure. And besides, you and dad aren't even divorced. And why him and not you?

I would never say this out loud, of course, but boy am I mad at her. I know everything I need to know, they assure me. Still, a couple of years is long enough. I'm ready for some answers.

PASTOR LARRY DOESN'T SEEM TO MIND if I don't feel like talking. Sometimes we play The Ungame or other games only counselors have. Or I stretch out on the floor and pretend to be exhausted, unable to carry one side of a conversation. Mom sees Pastor Larry once a week, too. What do they talk about? Do they play The Ungame? Does she also lie down on the floor to avoid speaking?

Pastor Larry asks about school. Asking is his job, I know, but it's still annoying. I scored 73 on my math test. That's a fifteen-point improvement over the last one, but Miss Murray requires a parent signature for anything under 75, just to make sure they at home know how poorly I'm doing. I'm sick of getting yelled at, so I find my last test and use it as a model to forge mom's signature. Later, I'm called down to the principal's office; mom is there with the principal and Miss Murray, waiting for me, and mom is mortified. Pastor Larry knows this already. What does he want me to say?

No, it has nothing to do with dad leaving. I'd like to get good grades. I study. I'm just too stupid to get A's. It's hard to pay attention. I get bored. I daydream. I think about baseball, and Green Day, and girls — so many girls to think about.

Mom impressively convinces the administration not to suspend me. We go home, and she breaks down as soon as the front door is shut. She's crying; Harold licks her hand. What can she do to help me, she wants to know. I tell her I don't know what's wrong with me. I'm just not smart, I say, and I have trouble concentrating. But I *am* smart, mom insists, and I do *not* have attention problems. She says she's sorry she and dad don't live together, and that she can't fathom how hard it must be on me, and that we need to pray every day that dad will come home and live with us again. I don't tell her this, but dad has nothing to do with it.

And now he's here, and we're sitting together in the family room, mom and me on the couch, Harold at her feet, and dad in the chair. They're going to help me make some changes. Rewards for good grades, and new punishments for bad grades. And here's a fifteen-page article on "Developing Effective Study Habits" for me to read.

It was a freaking 73. Not even failing.

And he left us! Why is he here? Why did you call him and tell him my business? Why do you two only ever unite when I screw up?

You let Davina do whatever she wants. Maybe you should start paying attention to her once in a while.

Get me out of here! I can't stand to see you right now, mom. I hate this. I hate living here. I'm not smart anymore. Deal with it!

Eventually they've said everything they'd planned on saying and I'm let loose. I run outside and get into dad's car, because he's going to take me away from mom for the next couple of hours. Maybe I can move in with dad permanently. I'll miss Harold, but I can see him when I come back for visits.

Maybe we can stop for ice cream. Maybe we can go to Blockbuster and rent a movie.

But, what's going on? Why does he have my backpack? I don't have any homework. He wants me to study. For what? I don't have a test tomorrow. Study in general? What's the point of going to dad's house if I have to put up with the same crap as at mom's?

At the stop sign, I get out of the car and make a break for it. Dad gets out after me and I hear him slam the door. His legs are longer than mine, and soon, his outstretched arm grabs the back of my shirt. The neckline momentarily chokes me before I'm spun around. Helpless, I collapse to escape his grip, but he pins my shoulders to the pavement in the middle of the street. I'm kicking, fighting to free myself, crying, screaming –

I hate you! I hate my life! Why won't you just leave me alone!

But Pastor Larry already knows what happened. I tell him it has nothing to do with the divorce. And anyway, they're not even divorced, just separated, although I admit for the first time I no longer think they might get back together. I don't care what they do anymore, as long as they leave me out of it.

"If you don't care," Pastor Larry says, "then why did you cry?"

"Because I'm stupid," I tell him. "They think I'm smart, but I'm not. I wish they would just accept that and move on."

"DANNY, HONEY, I KNOW THIS IS HARD. Your grades haven't been the same since dad left, but you need to find a way. I know it's hard not having dad here, but the Lord doesn't give us anything we can't handle. Every night I pray that he'll come back home to us. Until that happens, you have to be strong."

Dad left at the end of fourth grade; fifth grade was the first year I didn't get straight A's. The next year was slightly better, but seventh grade was worse, and this year is looking to be a new low. I peaked early, it looks like.

"It's just a coincidence," I tell her.

I wish she would shut up. Joel is outside waiting for me so we can hit fly balls to each other. Harold will run back and forth between us, chasing the ball no matter how high in the air it goes. Mom brought Harold to our baseball game once, but he got loose and ran onto the field, and the game was held up for ten minutes while everyone chased after him, before Joel dove and caught his leash. I thought it was funny, but mom was embarrassed and dad was angry. I used to think Harold might've driven dad away. I was so stupid back then. But sometimes I wonder.

Fortunately, mom isn't committed to our conversation. She'd like to get dinner in the oven. Dad will be here in an hour. Davina is home from college and doesn't have plans for the evening, so it'll be the four of us at the table. Afterward, dad will leave, and I'll go with him.

SWEET GUM TREE

BRAD AND I STAND IN MY LIVING ROOM and face the front door. My nine-month-old daughter is napping in the nursery. I'm holding a baseball bat. Brad holds a chainsaw.

"We're not overreacting, right?" I ask.

"No."

Brad is several inches taller than me, a good fifty pounds heavier, and has a punching bag in his backyard. He has started a tree-cutting and stump-removal business, and I rarely see him without either a chainsaw, an axe, or a lawnmower. Sometimes a dump truck drops off twenty-foot tree logs that take over his front yard.

"If they're looking for you," I said, "why would they come here?"

"Probably won't."

"I'm just saying we could probably sit down."

"You can if you want."

I'm a pianist. Brad and I like the same football team, and we both watch *The Walking Dead*. Otherwise we don't have much in common.

"So," I begin, still standing. "The Steelers, huh."

"TJ Watt is a beast."

Our longest interaction was the day he and his wife moved in next door. We also talked when I borrowed a drill from him to hang a picture and returned it an hour later. I didn't know how to stop the water one time when my boiler sprung a leak, and he helped me out. We also usually say "hi" when we see each other. It hasn't been much, but I've come to think of him as one of the nicest people I've ever met. His house has Steelers curtains in the front windows, visible from the road. When I went over to borrow his drill, I saw framed *Walking Dead* posters hanging inside.

It looks like we're having a conversation today.

"In the event of the zombie apocalypse," I say, gesturing toward his chainsaw, and recalling his axe and saws, "I feel pretty good about being your neighbor."

"I got you covered."

A black Escalade goes by. There are only twelve houses on this calm street. Other than a pair of retired nuns in the house on the other side of Brad's and a mild-mannered chubby gay guy a little further down, the neighborhood is filled with middle-aged divorced women. I rarely hear anything but the slamming of car doors and Brad's chainsaw. An Escalade stands out. This is the second time I've seen it drive by today. I can't tell if Brad noticed.

Brad is a stay-at-home dad like me. His baby daughter was born a few days after they moved in, so she must be four months old. I guess that's another thing we have in common. I'll have to remember that if we're struggling for a topic later.

"Joann working?" he asks.

"She's usually home by four. There's plenty of time to do whatever we're doing." I shrug. "Where's your little girl?"

"Grandparents," he says. "With Kate. Back next week."

The dumped-off pile of wood on his front lawn is an eyesore, but it will all be gone in a few days. Usually he's limited to working on it weekends or evenings after Kate can take over baby duty. Brad is dedicated. He'll work nonstop during that hour and a half till it gets too dark to see.

Because I rarely see him without one, I was only a little alarmed earlier when I opened the door to Brad and a chainsaw. An hour later, he still hasn't put it down. He'd been out on a job. Even with all his ropes and pulleys, Brad had lost control of a thick two-hundred pound branch that crashed into the house through a window and hit his employer's wife. She was alive, but bloody, and pissed. Once she pieced together what had happened, she started screaming at Brad and threatened much worse than a lawsuit. Brad is convinced that her husband is a major player in organized crime. That was the most I'd ever heard him talk, which is why part of me thinks it's true. It can't be true, though. We live in southern Virginia. There's crime, yes, but it's not organized.

"You doing anything today?" he asks.

"I have rehearsal tonight," I say, nodding toward my piano.

"What's that?"

"I'm the music director at Christ Episcopal. We have choir practice Wednesday nights. I direct the choir."

"You sing?"

"Not really," I say. "But these little churches aren't very particular, especially since I play piano too, and they get to pay one person to do two jobs."

The church is my main gig. I also teach piano lessons Tuesday and Thursday evenings. It doesn't add up to full-time, but the rest of the time I'm a father.

I have the sudden urge to hammer or drill something, to prove my manhood in front of Brad. Instead, I hear my baby girl waking up, and I need to get a bottle ready.

I'm surprised she slept this long, though I had hoped the game Brad and I were playing would be over by the time she woke up. There's a bag of breast milk on the kitchen counter that I took out of the freezer earlier to thaw. I pour it into a bottle and swish it around. Back in the living room, for the first time since coming over, Brad has put his chainsaw down by his feet. He has also helped himself to my daughter and is lightly rocking her in his huge arms.

Silently, he takes the bottle from my hand and gently places the rubber nipple in the sleepy little girl's mouth.

"It's like looking into the future," he says of my daughter, roughly five months older than his. "God, I love babies. Don't you?"

IN THE BACKYARD MY LITTLE GIRL crawls around on the freshly cut grass. I have a well-groomed lawn I hope Brad will acknowledge. It is mid-afternoon and we're way overdue for lunch. I have fired up the grill for a couple of burgers. Brad has brought his chainsaw out with him, as I have brought my baseball bat. He has already admired my Steelers grill spatula. It occurs to me that the metal edges of the spatula might do more damage than the blunt barrel of my baseball bat, though the spatula is shorter.

Brad has cut down the lower branches of his sweet gum tree, but when the wind blows, the sweet gum balls from the remaining branches still drop into my backyard. The bulk fall over the winter, but I find them all year round. They are the size of golf balls, spiky, and a nuisance. I pick up a gum ball from the ground and show Brad.

"When are you going to finish cutting down that tree?" I ask, though I know he has every right to leave it up.

"They land in your yard?" Brad says. "I'll get on that." He looks up at the tree, as if he hasn't thought about it in a while. "Maybe this weekend."

Brad stays close to the house, so it's on me to periodically glance around the side to see if anyone's there. I hadn't realized Brad is such a softie for babies. It's killing him to keep from running out into the yard to lift the baby up in the air and blow on her tummy. His eyes are glued to her, except when he sees me drift off to the side, for a look at the street.

"A black Escalade keeps driving by," I say. "I've seen it four or five times already."

"That's them," Brad says.

I only see Brad's baby girl when he carries her, buckled up in her car seat, from the house to his truck. She rides in the front seat with him. I thought there were restrictions for children riding in the front seat before a certain age or under a certain height. Maybe it doesn't apply if your truck doesn't have a backseat.

I glance at the coals in the grill. They're just about ready. I grab a stick to spread them around a bit, then I throw on the burgers. They sizzle.

"There's the Escalade again," I say, walking back and forth.

Brad's truck is out front, so it looks like he's home. If what he believes is true, I don't know what they're waiting for. He and I have never been close, and under normal circumstances there would be no reason for him to be over here. He's never been before, anyway.

"And again," I say as the Escalade circles back. "They're getting more frequent."

The Escalade stops. My heart skips a beat, and I jump backwards before cautiously peering around the corner. The sun glares from its windows, and from this angle I can't see inside.

"It's just sitting there," I loudly whisper to Brad.

His instinct is to protect the baby. He scoops her up with one hand and, with the chainsaw in the other, bolts back into the house. I grab my baseball bat and follow them, though suddenly my shoes feel like lead.

Brad has my front door open a crack and is peeping through it. I notice his chainsaw has been set down on the coffee table, but my baby girl is still on his right arm.

"They're idling," he says.

"Maybe they want you to come out," I say, now desperate to get this over.

He glances at me and is mildly alarmed by the look on my face. "Stay calm. What would you normally be doing?"

I force a shrug. I look at the baby in his arms. I look around the house. "Probably playing piano."

"Play some."

Brad and the baby are in sight as I sit down at the piano and play the opening arpeggios of Mozart's *Fantasy in d minor*. I've occasionally assigned this piece to my better high school students. I make it to the first cadenza, and I start to feel better. I rip through the cadenza and hit the final high note harder than usual. I pause for dramatic effect.

"They're getting out," Brad says.

I feel sick.

"There's two of them. I can't tell if anyone else is in the car. It's turned off, anyway. You can keep playing."

"I don't feel up to it."

"I can't get a good look at them. Can you go out there?"

"Are you crazy?"

He looks back again. I have repossessed my baseball bat, and I'm holding it up, standing like I'm waiting for the pitcher to get set and deliver.

"Pretend to get the mail," he says. "Get a look inside the car. Maybe size them up."

I shuffle toward the door.

"Leave this," he says, taking the bat from me with the hand not holding a baby. "You don't need it. Just get the mail."

I brush past him and the baby and stand on the

porch for a second, looking away from his house and the goons. I step down and lose my footing, but I regain my balance before falling to the ground. Inside the mailbox are several envelopes. I close the mailbox and look at the Escalade. I have a good angle and can see clearly through the back window. Unless someone is lying down, there's no one else. I look over at Brad's house. The two men are standing on his door stoop, and they are looking at me.

"Hello," I say. "You friends of Brad?"

One of them is the classic henchman: big, ripped, bald, and silent. The other guy is smaller than me. The little guy says, "That's his truck, right?"

I look at Brad's truck, parked on the street in front of the Escalade, as if Brad wanted them to see it. I nod. "But they have another car, too."

"You haven't seen him?"

"Not today."

I've done my duty, and I head back inside. I sit down at the piano and pick the Mozart up where I left off. The second cadenza doesn't go as well, and I pause this time to breathe deep and calm my nerves.

"There's no one else in the car," I say.

I play some more of the *Fantasy*, but stop before it modulates to the major key. I'm not feeling major.

"They're inside," Brad says.

"Call the police!" I say. "That's breaking and

entering."

"I'm going over."

I don't argue. He takes a step outside before remembering to swap my baby for his chainsaw. Then he leaves, and I watch him walk across my lawn and through piles of logs, kindling, and sawdust. I'm relieved that he's gone, and ashamed for feeling that way. I listen closely but don't hear anything. The street is quiet. No one is slamming a car door. Brad isn't using his chainsaw. It's unsettling. I don't know how much time has passed when I hear my daughter whimpering.

Baby in hand, my turn to protect her, I walk through the house to the backyard. I use my Steelers grill spatula to jam the burnt remains of the burgers through the cracks and into the coals. I'm not hungry anymore, anyway.

"It's taken care of," Brad says as he reappears from around the corner of the house. He doesn't have his chainsaw. "Glad the wife is out of town." He looks at the charred meat patties, now in flames. "Forgot about those." He walks over to us and touches the baby's cheek, but I refuse to let go.

My eyes drift around the corner of my house and see the Escalade parked on the street.

"It's still there," I say.

"Have to move the car," he says. "But that's all right."

I notice specks of red on his shirt and face.

"Where are they?"

He contemplates a response. "There's still work to be done. Always is. But you're all set. Sorry about the burgers."

He turns around and heads home.

"I'll take care of that tree for you," he calls back.

In my arms, the baby pushes against my chest, ready to get down. I want to cradle her tight, but she is deceptively strong. Her gaze drifts toward Brad's house. She whines; I'm tired. I lower her to the ground and she takes off on all fours around the grassy back-yard. She is aiming for another sweet gum ball. I race to remove it from her path so she won't stab herself with its spikes. I fling the gum ball into Brad's back-yard. It hurts a little.

NOT LEAVING WITHOUT MY BOY

WHEN I SEE MY BOY AGAIN, he's potty-trained. I have mixed feelings about this. On one hand, I want to be a part of his milestones. On the other, it never sounded like fun.

In chronological order, the reasons they locked me up in the first place:

1. I knocked groceries out of a stranger's hands at the store.
2. I said the f-word to a pastor in his church.
3. I broke my brother-in-law's nose.
4. I beat up a guy outside the 7-Eleven.

That last one I don't think I would believe if they hadn't shown me the footage from the surveillance camera. I half-suspect the video was doctored up with CGI and that I was framed. The dude was twice my size.

I do remember punching my brother-in-law, though.

———

"I DON'T THINK IT'S ANYTHING TO BE PROUD of," Seth says, "that piece of garbage he made. Jason is family and all, but I'm embarrassed to be related to him."

"Seth!" his wife scolds.

We've finished eating and are sitting around the table, trying to recreate the family-centric life I'd had before the accident, and before the so-called piece of garbage. Everyone is making an effort to show I'm still part of the family except Seth, who's talking like I'm not there.

"I'm sorry, but that's just the way I feel," Seth says. "And I know you agree with me." He gestures toward his parents. "I'm sick of everyone tip-toeing around him like he's the only one suffering."

"I guess you didn't learn compassion in seminary," I say, getting up from the table.

"What is the matter with you?" my mother-in-law says to Seth. To me, she says "Please stay."

"Sweetie, it's time to go," I call. Robby comes bounding from the living room.

"You don't have to leave," my mother- and father-in-law say at the same time.

"She was my sister," Seth continues. "Not just for a few years, but my *entire* life. And no one feels sorry for me."

Seth's wife continues scolding while I do my best to ignore everyone and get Robby's shoes and coat on.

"And that...thing of his?" Seth goes on. "That's what did it. It's out there. That's what killed her. You, Jason," he points at me. "You should be ashamed of yourself, promoting something like that."

"Back off," I warn. I brush past him and grab my keys from the table.

"You're not the only one," he repeats. "I don't think I'll ever forgive you."

"Read your Bible," I say, getting in his face. "Then say that. And climb off your high horse."

He is not intimidated. "Enjoy your blood money," he says.

I pop him. He jolts back several steps and falls down. Lying on the floor, he starts bleeding right away. No one is upset with me. Even his wife is reluctant to come to his aid.

"Okay, honey, you ready to go?" I say.

Robby holds on to my hand as we walk outside, and I strap him into his car seat. Within a week, a guy will bump into me outside of the 7-Eleven. I will send him to the hospital, and then I will be committed.

I AM MOVED INTO AN APARTMENT close to my in-laws' house, an apartment I used to live in. It is also close to where they work and go to church, and where I used to go to church. They can keep an eye on me this way. I'm not allowed to drive, but at least it's not far from the grocery store.

Some of my best memories happened here: coming home to it at the end of our honeymoon, pretending to care about the color of the drapes while all along letting her get what she wanted, so many great talks, so much laughing, coming home from work to her embrace, receiving the phone call when the contract was finalized, how proud she was of me, where Robby was conceived.

This is cruel and sadistic, but my own parents were in on the decision, so I'm not too bitter.

"We didn't bring everything," my father explains to me as I move in. "You and I can drive back to your house sometime and pick some more things up, if you want. But I know you like to watch movies, so we brought your TV. And I know you'll want to read, so we brought your books."

I don't know if I'll ever go back. They left my couch and bed and other furniture down there. Someone has scrounged up a recliner, though, and a twin bed for the bedroom.

"I don't mind making another trip down there," my father repeats. "With you."

It's not so bad really, and I handle it okay. Without my wife's touch, the inside doesn't resemble our honeymoon cottage from years ago.

The day after I move in, my father-in-law shows up at the door and invites me over to see my boy. It's part of the arrangement. My in-laws have

Robby and I can't show up unannounced. They will also drive me to my sessions and check up on me once a day. I'm not under house arrest, but it's sort of like a halfway house, like I'm out on parole and can't go too far and have to be back by a certain time.

We enter, and I can hear him on the other side of the house. He's reading books with his grandma. He has most of the books memorized but he has trouble with his consonants and not all of the words sound right. I cross the house. He looks up at me and smiles.

"Hey, sweetie," I say. I crouch down and invite him into my arms. "How's my little guy?"

"It's dada," my mother-in-law says. "Say 'hi, dada.' Go give dada a hug."

"Can I have a hug, honey?" I say. "Come here."

"It's been a few months," my father-in-law says. "He's probably a little confused."

"Give him a minute to get used to you again," my mother-in-law says.

I spread my arms out, still inviting a hug. "How's my little sweetie guy?"

Robby doesn't budge from my mother-in-law's lap. He clings to her a little bit.

"He's just confused," my father-in-law says again. "He'll come around. He just doesn't understand."

Robby resents having had to watch me get carted away in a police car. He resents having been passed around by strangers in uniform as they figured out what to do with him.

BETWEEN THE LIFE INSURANCE and the royalties, I'm not going to have to work for a while. I watch a lot of movies. I watch the long movies, the kind with built-in intermissions, like *Once Upon a Time in America*, and *Gone With the Wind*, and *Novecento*.

My father-in-law stops by Sunday morning to take me to church, but I'm still in bed. I don't want to face the pastor.

AFTER THE ACCIDENT I DON'T GO HOME for a month. My mother-in-law is working a silent auction fundraiser, held in the church fellowship hall. She's also volunteering to watch Robby, to give me a break. She says the auction isn't really work. Plus she loves parading her grandson around.

Robby and I get there after the silent auction has already started. She's on the far side of the room and doesn't see me, so I figure I'll pop in and out. But the pastor stops me at the door and says everyone needs to pay admission, which is in actuality how they raise most of the money.

"I'm just dropping my boy off," I say. I'm holding Robby in my right arm. "His grandma is right over there."

"I'm sorry, but you'll have to wait here," the

pastor says. "It's a fundraiser."

"But I'm not here for the auction."

"Everyone needs to pay admission," he repeats.

I don't like this guy. I used to listen to him every Sunday morning, but he doesn't know who I am, even after he did the funeral. And he called Robby "Bobby" in the eulogy.

"Just, God, get out of the way," I say.

"Excuse me?" he says, taken aback.

"Why don't you go stand way over there for ten minutes, all right?" I say. "Then, when you come back, I'll be gone."

He stares and doesn't say anything.

"Back the fuck off!"

I push my way past him. I put Robby down, and he races toward his grandma. She didn't see what happened and doesn't know why he's upset. I should leave, but I'm feeling rebellious, so I stick around to talk with my mother-in-law for a minute, and I look at some of the items up for auction before seeing the pastor coming, pointing at me, followed by a couple of big guys acting as bouncers. So I bounce myself.

MY BROTHER-IN-LAW, SETH, stops by to see me, unannounced, saving his parents from a day of checking up on me.

"I don't blame you," he says. "I'm so ashamed

of how I acted. We're family, Jason, you and me, so I'm going to stick by you. I hope you'll do the same."

Seth tells me what he's been up to in the months since I broke his nose. He is now a part-time church youth leader.

"I needed therapy, too," he says. "I had some anger I needed to sort through. I was angry at God. I didn't understand His will. I was short-sighted. I was seeing someone for a while, too, like you were. We prayed a lot together. It really helped. Do you want to pray together?"

"No."

"Do you want me to refer you to my guy?"

"I have a guy."

I enjoy my sessions. I've always loved talking about myself, but no one wanted to listen before. Now they listen. Nobody blames me for acting the way I did. It was wrong, but they understand. I always wanted to put family first. Maybe I lost sight of things. On the verge of swelling to a family of four, instead we are a family of two.

SOME OLD FRIENDS STOP BY. I've seen Joe twice. He says he knows someone who is dying to meet me. She teaches at his school. I tell Joe I wouldn't mind meeting her. I could use being adored.

I don't have a car, but after we talk for twenty minutes she says she'll pick me up. We go to a comedy club called the Loony Bin. The sign says *Escape Reality*. I haven't laughed so much in a while.

She's a laugher, too, as it turns out. She laughs at all the comics' jokes. She laughs at my jokes, too, even though I'm not funny. She asks me tons of questions. She wants to know everything about me.

We go to bed together. She doesn't stay the night because she hasn't brought anything and she has to get up early the next morning for work. She stops by the next morning, though, at 6:30, on her way to school, and we do it again. At the end of the school day, she calls and says she's coming over. I haven't gotten out of bed, so I crawl out to take a shower and make myself presentable, but she's calling from my doorstep and showers with me. She stays the night and the weekend. It's crowded on my single bed. She gets dirty looks when my in-laws stop by to take me over to see Robby.

She's only the second girl I've ever been with.

The obsessed fan thing gets old after a week. I start hating her and break it off.

I meet Anthony. We go out to eat and have a nice time. I see Joe and his wife at the restaurant. Anthony gets up for the men's room.

"I never heard you mention him before," Joe says.

"This is a date," I say. "So be cool."

I can barely handle Joe's reaction, and I'm

thankful his wife is out of earshot.

Anthony drives me home, and we shake hands as I get out of the car.

The next week he brings a six-pack over, and we watch *Monster*. When it's over I lean in to kiss him, and he pulls back.

"What are you doing?" he says.

"Aren't you gay?" I say.

"Yeah. But you're not."

Anthony leaves, and I drink the beers he's left behind in the refrigerator. I'm a lightweight, and I get drunk. I walk over to my in-laws' house. It's dark and all the lights are off, but their cars are in the driveway, so I know they're home.

"Let me in!" I shout. "Let me in! I have a right to be here! You have my son and I want him! Give me my son and I'll leave!" I pound the door with my fists. "Goddammit, you can't do this to me! Fucking open the door and let me in! He's all I have! Give him to me! Robby! Can you hear me? Robby! Come to dada! Come to your dada, sweetie! Fucking come to me! I'm your fucking father! Motherfuckers! He's mine! He's fucking mine! Open the goddamn fucking door!"

I pick up a rock the size of a softball from the garden and heave it through the kitchen window.

———

I'M IN CHURCH and the pastor I said the f-word to shakes my hand and says that it's good to see me and "Bobby", and that the door to his office is always open.

"As long as you pay admission," he says, laughing, daring to joke about it.

"It's Robby," I say, but he's gone, too far to hear me.

I go with my mother-in-law to get Robby out of Sunday school, and then everyone has dinner together, like the old days, almost.

"Here, dada," Robby says to me. I'm sitting at the dining room table. We've finished eating.

"Books," Robby says.

"Yeah?" I say. "You want dada to read to you? You want to read about the duckies?"

I sit down on the floor, Robby sits on my lap, and we read about the duckies. My mother-in-law is smiling. She gets her camera and takes a picture.

Robby and I run around in the backyard. I pick him up and swing him around. I put him on my shoulders. He climbs on my back like I'm a horse. I tickle him, and he belly-laughs so hard he gets the hiccups. At least one person watches us at all times.

At first, my father-in-law insists on driving me home when Robby goes down for a nap. That's the rule. But it's a nice day, so he lets me walk.

I walk into the grocery store to pick up a few things. Someone's cart is blocking an entire aisle.

Instead of giving her attitude about it, I wait patiently for her to move. It's inconsiderate of her, but I'm not getting into trouble again. That's what happened before.

THIS GUY GRABS A HANDFUL of things off a shelf. I'm going down the aisle with a cart, and he backs up without looking, and I run into him with my cart.

"Watch where you're going," he says to me.

"Where *I'm* going?" I say. "You're the idiot walking backwards."

"Excuse me?" he says

I step forward and bat the groceries out of his hands. I chuck eggs at his chest. Then I leave. Everyone blows it way out of proportion. Nothing would've happened, probably, if my mother-in-law hadn't seen me go into the store and hadn't been catching up to me to see how I was doing and all that good crap. That was horrible luck, but I'm over it. People are self-centered, and that's just the way it is.

BESIDES MY TIME WITH ROBBY, MY sessions are the most fun I have. After each session, I feel like the doctor is my friend, and I want to ask him to hang out later, or maybe go to a ballgame on the weekend. But I know it's his job to be my friend. He sure is good at it. I think he genuinely likes me. I think all my doctors have liked me. We have good discussions. I open up to them and we make each other laugh. I never lose my temper, either. The whole time I was locked up, I never raised my voice and never hit anyone or anything, not even a wall or a pillow. In the beginning I was a little frustrated because they kept showing me the surveillance video, and they kept saying the person in it was me. It looked like me, but I feel like I would remember something like that. Finally I told them that I sort of remember it, but it's blurry, and I don't remember too many details. That satisfied them a little.

I look at my books. If I read something I've already read, then I know I will like it. If I read something new, I might not. I don't know what to read.

I walk to my in-laws, uninvited but in my right mind, to see Robby. This is against the rules, but I've been good and I deserve it. No one comes to the door, though, or answers the phone, and there aren't any cars in the driveway. I sit outside the door for a long time before giving up and walking home.

On the way home I walk through the cemetery. I find the plot, sit down, and stare. I don't cry, though. It's worse than crying. It's all the emotional turmoil of crying without the actual release. It's numbing. And it's most of the time.

———

MY FATHER-IN-LAW STOPS BY every Sunday in hopes of luring me to church, and for the third Sunday in a row, I'm ready when he rings the doorbell. I'm a model son-in-law.

I notice people's stares. I'm not used to them. I'm not sure if they stare because they feel sorry for me, because they think I'm a ticking time bomb, or because of my celebrity status, like they can't believe I can show my face in a church. Someday I'll go to a church where nobody knows me.

The pastor goes out of his way to say hello to me again. He asks about "Bobby" and I don't correct him. He says I'm fortunate to have such wonderful in-laws, and I agree. I talk for a little bit with someone I knew in college while my mother-in-law fetches Robby from Sunday school. We're still lingering outside the sanctuary when Robby sees me.

"Dada!" He races for me, and I time his arrival perfectly, picking him up and lifting him high over my head. He giggles and then belly-laughs.

"How's my little sweetie guy?" I say. "How's my boy?" I hug him tight and give him kisses on the cheeks.

My in-laws look happy, pleased, even proud of themselves.

"I thought I would take Robby out to lunch," I say. "Some father and son bonding time. Just the two of us."

"You know you can't do that," my father-in-law says.

"What's the big deal? I've been good. We'll just go right down the street here."

"Don't do this," he says. His smile is gone now. "If you want to be re-evaluated, that's fine, we can arrange for a re-evaluation this week. But it's not going to be today."

"Who cares about that?" I say. "You're as smart as those guys. You know what you see. I'm fine. Robby and I are great together. Nothing's going to happen if he's with me. I at least have *that* much control."

"He *was* with you when *it* happened," my mother-in-law says.

I still don't totally believe that *it* actually happened. The guy was twice my size. And I'd punched very few people in my day.

"Come on," I plead. "You don't know it's going to happen again. I feel great. I'm perfectly fine."

"I'm sorry, Jason, but we have to say no."

"This is ridiculous," I say. I put Robby down, and he clings to his grandma's leg. "He's my son."

"And he's *our* grandson."

"This is fucking ridiculous!" I repeat. Some remaining church lingerers gasp.

"Don't say that, Jason. That's not who you are."

"I'm a grown man. I can do what I want."

"All right," my father-in-law says, trying to coax me outside. "Let's go."

"I'm not fucking leaving without my boy!"

"I'm sorry," the pastor says, walking up behind me, "but I need you to watch your language and keep your voice down."

"We have this under control," my father-in-law tells him.

I glare at the pastor. "What's his name," I say, pointing at Robby. I reach out and snatch Robby's arm, yanking him over to me. Robby starts to cry. I give the pastor my most violent look. "What's his name!? You fucking idiot!"

"You're not helping yourself," my father-in-law says calmly.

My mother-in-law tries to take Robby back. "Jason, you're hurting him!" she cries.

"You are going to have to leave!" the pastor says, more sternly this time.

Robby is crying and people are staring. I let go of Robby's arm and he buries his face in his grandma's lap. There are marks on his arm where my grip had been. My father-in-law gently guides me around to face the exit. But I pull away, pivot, and nail the pastor in the face.

———

IT'S A HALF-HOUR BEFORE CHURCH. It takes less than five minutes to walk there. We've been packing up our tiny apartment and there are moving boxes everywhere. My wife weaves her way into the kitchen and sits at the table. I set her breakfast down in front of her and kiss the top of her head.

"Are you feeling all right?" I ask.

"I feel like a lucky wife," she says.

"How's our little Robby boy?" I say. I pat her rounding tummy.

I sit down on the other side of the table and admire her. This is what I want. This is the way it's supposed to be.

I'M BACK NOW. Some of the faces are the same, but not everyone remembers me. I've had some visitors. My parents have come a couple times, and Joe once. My in-laws have come also. They say I can see Robby when I get out. That'll be a few months.

RULES FOR PROCREATION

KIM USES SEVERAL PILLOWS to prop Ora Lee's legs into the air. She hopes this will increase the odds of conception. This is an old wives' tale, Kim knows, but she's willing to try anything before she becomes an old wife herself. Tucker is getting dressed in the corner when he hears a commotion outside.

The Harrises are losing custody of their son, Tucker sees, peaking through the blinds. Mr. Harris hangs his head in shame while Mrs. Harris's wailing is heard throughout the neighborhood. The boy is shoved into the child services vehicle. Several neighbors restrain Mrs. Harris from pounding on the car's windows and chasing after it down the street. The boy is gone, and the neighborhood's only African-American family is left without a child. When all is hopeless, Mrs. Harris turns to her husband. She shrieks and screams, kicks and slaps. Mr. Harris raises his chin to accept the blame, giving his wife a better angle to more easily bloody his face.

Now fully dressed, Tucker joins Kim outside the Blaylock residence to watch the scene while Ora Lee remains in bed relaxing her reproductive muscles.

"I started this," a spectator brags, filling them in. "I seen the black boy's daddy smack 'im in the face. I tol' Peacemaker Kopf about it yesterday while he was makin' his rounds. Zero tolerance for hittin' a child. And now they lose the privilege of havin' one."

This is far from an everyday occurrence. And having a child is indeed a privilege coveted by many. Dr. and Mrs. Blaylock, for instance, tried unsuccessfully for years to adopt a child.

Later, Kim seeks out Mrs. Harris to confirm the story the old-fashioned way, first-hand. They don't even believe in spanking, Mrs. Harris claims. But the child took the Lord's name in vain, and her husband lost control. Four fingers across the child's cheek; that was all.

"He would never harm a hair on that boy's head," she says, quietly, her initial sobbing subsided. "Never before, and, I believe with all my heart, never again."

The fine print of the adoption laws prohibits homosexual couples from adopting, the discovery of which caused waves throughout many households. Kim and Ora Lee cried for days. Where the Harris boy will end up, nobody knows. But because Tucker too has lost a child, this is a particularly traumatic incident for the triangle.

The kitchen has been remodeled since a combination of a house fire and sleeping pills left Tucker without a family. It was in this kitchen where Kim, a longtime friend of Tucker's and his wife's, first awk-wardly proposed that he father a child for her and Ora Lee. Too much silence followed. Kim wasn't sure Tucker had been with a woman since his wife and new-born died. Afraid he was going to say no, she was about to resort to jokes – "I'm whoring my wife out to you for free" – when he agreed.

From inside and through the kitchen window, Tucker sees his neighbor push his son. Mr. White uses only one hand for the push, and the boy awkwardly shuffles his feet to maintain balance. The boy steps for-ward to again annoy his father, and this time he is met with both palms. Stumbling in reverse, the boy loses equilibrium, falls backward, and hits his head on a stump. The boy sits up and vomits. Through the win-dowpane, Tucker can hear the boy's father shouting, and the boy crying.

SOON THIS STREET WILL BE GONE. With the in-creased driving restrictions and higher automotive taxes, few people bother to own cars. Out-of-the-way residential streets like this one are in line to be ripped up and replaced by a footpath.

Derrick Kopf walks the beat. A slow pace al-lows attention to detail and affords opportunities for conversation. He will ask questions of those sitting on their porches, but he won't step foot on anyone else's property without an invitation, because that would be trespassing, and he is a stickler for the rules.

"Too many goddamned people on this planet," Kopf was known to say. "It'd be easier to just wipe a bunch of 'em out. But nobody wants to get their hands dirty and make the decision. I'll do it; I don't care. Give me the power and I'll gladly push the button."

Kopf nominated himself to form and lead the Peacemakers, one of hundreds of government-registered Citizen Surveillance groups throughout the country that enforce laws too small to matter to the police or the military, most of whom have their hands tied with the riots downtown. The real police haven't been seen here in this neighborhood in months. Kopf was so passionate that he quit his day job to voluntarily fight crime full-time. Justice is its own reward.

He takes joy in recruiting enthusiastic new Peacemakers. But even when a man turns down his invitation to join the Peacemakers, the respect the rejecter showers upon Kopf makes up for it. Privately, he loves being addressed as Peacemaker Kopf.

This Tucker fella doesn't say much. In greeting Tucker, Kopf has received only a head nod, a half-hearted wave, or occasionally a "Hi Derrick" if Tucker is distracted. Kopf is aware that Tucker lost his family, and he isn't sure he wants to recruit him, anyway, but he would at least like to get a few words out of him — a sentence, even a fragment, anything that could be construed as an invitation onto the porch.

This is by design, of course. Kopf is vain, and Tucker won't stroke his ego. However, himself overcome with a desire for justice, Tucker breaks his silence and approaches Kopf the next time he rounds the corner.

"When Mr. Harris slapped his son, it was an isolated incident. It's been weeks and they still haven't gotten their kid back. Compared to that, don't you think Mr. White should be in jail?"

Peacemaker Kopf nods as Tucker speaks. "But we don't know it was isolated."

"We don't know that it wasn't. With Mr. White we do know. I can swear to that."

"What makes you think it was isolated?"

"Kim is certain of it," Tucker says, pointing with his eyes toward the Blaylock house. "She's friendly with most people and knows the Harrises pretty well. Why? Are you saying it wasn't?"

"You spend a lotta time with those dykes, dontcha? I seen you over there more than once. Y'all pretty close?"

Kopf's language makes Tucker cringe, but he tries to hide it. And what is Kopf insinuating? He couldn't know what they've been up to, could he? Either way, anything more about Kim and Ora Lee would further shift the conversation away from the White house next door.

"Something needs to be done about White."

Kopf gestures toward the White house. Tucker turns and sees White watching them, though he is out of earshot. Kopf grins smugly, pushes back his shoulders, and sticks out his chest.

"Thank you for bringing this to the attention of the Peacemakers. We'll take it under advisement."

He sticks out his hand, and Tucker feels obligated to shake it.

THE NEW REGIME HAD CAMPAIGNED on a promise of compromise. The rallying cry of women's health groups protested the government's intrusion into women's uteruses, so the government got into men's scrotums. This, the new regime announced, made for an even playing field. Compromise, they boasted.

Tucker's wife gave birth to and brought home a healthy baby boy. At this time, men were given a three-month grace period – in the event of a miscarriage, stillborn birth, or neonatal fatality – before having the mandatory vasectomy. Arguments ensued. Should a couple be allowed a second child if the first was born with severe mental or physical defects? For now, no. Nor could a couple conceive if either parent had previously – voluntarily or not - given up a child for adoption.

With the three-month grace period, however, too many accidents led to too many illegal children. The illegals were taken from their parents, but the orphanages were overcrowded, and because only certain childless couples were able to adopt, they would remain overcrowded for the foreseeable future. But now reverse vasectomies have been virtually perfected, and the law has been changed to require men to have the vas snipped as soon as their partners' pregnancies are reported. Because this law came later, however, Tucker is the rare man capable of fathering a child despite having already done so.

Gay marriage is legal by federal mandate, to the outrage of some, but gays cannot adopt, to the outrage of others – another compromise. Male-male couples are out of luck, while lesbian couples can take advantage of a loophole. Too many lesbians have been getting pregnant, however, so even more laws are in the works. The votes haven't been there so far, but every week new polls show that the efforts to outlaw these pregnancies are gaining support.

The day the Whites lose custody of their child goes a lot differently from the day the Harrises lost theirs. Mrs. White does not scream. Mr. White does not show remorse. Only those who recognize the CPA van from weeks earlier congregate to witness the White child's being taken into foster custody. Once the van is gone, the crowd disperses. Peacemaker Kopf and Mr. White shake hands before Kopf too departs.

Neither disgraced family has earned their child back by the time the leaves change color and begin to fall. Tucker continues to try to impregnate Ora Lee. Kim reads a theory that a man's sperm count is higher in the morning than at night. Kim and Ora Lee ask Tucker over before work, rather than in the evening, and Tucker sets his morning alarm fifteen minutes earlier.

Kim is in the room with them, kissing and caressing Ora Lee's face so the child will be conceived in love, although Tucker does care very much for both of them. Sometimes he lingers at the door and watches them before quietly slipping out, only to repeat the process the next day. Kim and Ora Lee will be happy to have Tucker play a role in raising the child. And the rare opportunity to father a child for a second time is certainly appealing.

He still has enough time to eat breakfast before catching the bus for work. The road between his house and the Blaylocks' has lines painted on it as the city prepares to dig it up as part of the Road Elimination Act. But standing amidst these lines is Mr. White. Tucker slows before seeing two more Peacemakers approaching from opposite directions. He stops. All are facing him, having just watched him exit the Blaylocks'. Tucker hears some rustling behind him where two more men, including Mr. Harris, appear from behind the house. Kim and Ora Lee's bedroom is on the first floor – it's a one-story house. Could they have peeked in?

"And what on God's green earth were you doin' in there, Tucker, m'boy?" White asks, grinning. This is White's mission, Tucker realizes, possibly his initiation. "Don't feel like talkin'?" White jeers. "What could you possibly be doin' with those ladies every single mornin'?"

"What's it to you?" Tucker dares to say.

"It's officially my duty to make sure this neigh-borhood is a law-abidin' neighborhood. And that's what I'm doin'. Just makin' sure. So y'all best answer the question."

Tucker doesn't answer and instead picks back up his pace and brushes past White. From inside his house, Tucker watches the five Peacemakers – has Mr. Harris really joined them? – convene at White's post. After some discussion and gesturing toward both Tucker's and the Blaylocks' houses, they part.

Tucker, like many others, doesn't own a car, with driving so expensive and so seldom permitted. On the bus, en route to work, Tucker calls Kim to tell her what happened.

"Unfortunately, I'm not surprised," Kim says. "I'm watching the news now. Very soon, maybe as early as next week, it will be officially illegal to do what we're doing. In fact, you're already illegal, you John you. As for the baby, if the date of conception is before the vote passes, then there's nothing they can do. But if conceived afterwards, we'll get in a shit-ton of trouble, and they'll take the baby away from us."

Tucker's heart sinks as he listens silently and attentively. "Then we'd better make the most of the time we have left."

"For real, I don't think there are more than a few days. The resistance in Congress is crumbling fast. Plus, in the meantime," Kim continues, "Citizen Sur-veillance has been mandated to do whatever they can to prevent it from happening, even before it's officially illegal."

"That doesn't make sense!"

"It's kind of fuzzy," Kim agrees. "But all this has to be what was motivating your White trash neighbor this morning."

"Right."

"Listen. I understand if another week's worth of getting off with the lesbian across the street isn't worth risking your life. Who knows, maybe one of your swimmers made it through this morning. But if not, I won't pressure you into it."

Kim pauses so long that Tucker knows she's waiting for him to respond. He swallows and breathes deeply.

"Well, it's been fun, I won't lie," he admits, anything to lighten the mood. "I love you," he says. "And I love Ora Lee. You're my family now, and I want this baby to be born. So, if you're leaving it up to me, let's keep trying."

"Oh my God, thank you so much," Kim gushes, fighting to keep her emotions in check. Back to business: "Then I'll plan on having you over tonight. Bring your A-game."

"Ora Lee is working tonight," Tucker reminds her, amused that he knows their schedules as well as he does.

"I'll be here," she said. "It's time to double

down. Maybe something's wrong with Ora Lee's plumbing; I don't know; they won't test for that anymore. But I think I'm ovulating now anyway, so we'll just have to chance it with my genes. Let me know when you're on your way, and I'll prep myself."

THE FIRST FEW TIMES they were turned down for adoption, Kim was convinced race was a factor. She threatened to file a discrimination suit before the adoption fine print was discovered.

Ora Lee took Kim's last name when they got married. She believed, and Kim agreed, that she would have difficulty building a practice as Dr. Chang. And indeed, as Dr. Blaylock, she has built a respectable practice, despite looking indisputably Asian, and losing only an occasional patient after a face-to-face meeting.

Despite the likelihood of future racial discrimination, however, they decided it would be Ora Lee's egg their child would grow from, because of a history of mental illness on Kim's side of the family. Now this precaution seems stupid. They both should have been trying with Tucker, and now Kim is kicking herself.

Kim is antsy. How selfish would it be to ask Tucker to leave work in the middle of the day to take care of business with her instead? She has little to do but wait for him. She eats nothing but fruit and drinks only water.

She goes for a walk around the neighborhood

and stops to visit Mr. Harris, who is working in his garage with the door open.

"How are you and your lovely wife? Ora Lee and I have been thinking about you."

"Fine, thanks," Mr. Harris responds curtly, not really looking up.

"Please tell me you're not working with the Peacemakers," she blurts out. He stops tinkering, but keeps his head down. His silence is Kim's answer. "How can you? They're a hate group."

"I'm just trying to get back my boy."

"What did they say you need to do?" she asks. "You're a good man, but you've been without your son for months now, while I hear that White asshole is getting his kid back next week. Are these really people you can trust?"

"Look, Kopf don't like you." He looks up and makes eye contact. "If you ask him, gay people are worse than us blacks. You've always been good to me, though, you and Ora Lee, and my wife likes you. So I'll do you this courtesy." He pauses, debating right and wrong versus self-interest. "Whatever's goin' on with you and that Tucker fella across the street, y'all'd better knock it off. Ever since Tucker turned in Mr. White, the guy's been out to get 'im. Don't tell me what y'all are up to; I don't want to know. But you'd better stop. It's not worth it."

"It's all gone wrong, hasn't it?" Kim says.

"Just gotta deal," he shrugs. "Don't talk to my wife anymore," he says. "And don't come here again."

TUCKER ARRIVES HOME promptly at five. He takes a quick shower, drinks a glass of water, and steps outside onto his porch. The neighborhood is silent; nobody in their yards, garages, or porches; nobody patrolling the streets. In his paranoia, he thinks he sees somebody hiding behind a tree, but when he looks a second time, nobody's there. Every other tree he eyes carefully. Nothing. He steps off the porch, crunches leaves as he crosses his yard, the street, and the Blaylocks' yard, and rings the doorbell.

Kim has been waiting for him. She swings the door open and abruptly pulls him inside.

"Don't stand there for everyone to see!" she scolds. She closes the door and peers out the windows on opposite sides of the house. "Looks good," she announces, lightly tapping him on the shoulder with her fist.

"I'm kind of nervous," he says.

"I'm nervous, too," she agrees, but grabs him by the hand and leads him to the bedroom.

It doesn't take long. Out of respect for the two of them, he has tried not to prolong the act, though with the increased frequency and the relative lack of intimacy lately with Ora Lee it has taken longer than would be ideal. With Kim, it is also passionless and mechanical, but the excitement of someone new speeds things along, and within a couple of minutes he ejaculates.

"Thank you," Kim says, half-naked on the bed while Tucker wipes and pulls his pants back on. "If you're up for it later, let's try again."

"Should be do-able," he says, turning to leave, trying to keep a straight face. Remedying the injustice to Kim and Ora Lee will, in part, help him fill the void left by the loss of his own family. Still, because he is a human male, it's hard to downplay how much he's been enjoying this.

"Stay a minute," she says. "You always leave so quickly." She gestures at the other side of the bed, and Tucker sits next to her.

"I wish I could feel whether or not it's working," she says, raising her bare legs high into the air. "How long did it take for you and your wife to conceive?"

Tucker shrugs. "Maybe a week?"

"Really?"

"It was kind of shocking how quickly we got pregnant," he laughs.

"Damn, lucky bitch," she says, missing her old friend. "Well, we've decided if it's a boy we're naming him after you."

There is a pounding and a slam from the front of the house. Kim springs off of the bed, seamlessly pulls on a pair of sweats, and bolts from the room.

"Get out!" Kim screams. Tucker's instinct is to follow her and come to her defense before realizing Kim was addressing *him,* telling *him* to get out.

He likely has only a few seconds. Because both the front and back doors are surely blocked, he closes the door and scans the bedroom in a panic for a hiding place – the closet, under the bed – before deciding to go out the window. He has trouble getting the screen to lift, so he punches it out, and it softly clangs to the ground, cushioned by leaves and mulch. He climbs out, scraping his shins on the metal window frame, and drops to the ground, thankful now that the bedroom is on the first floor. He hears shouting. He closes the window behind him and ducks behind the bushes.

Footsteps in the leaves precede Mr. White's voice: "Where's that piece a shit at?" They run by, but fearing they may double back, Tucker stays put, crouching as low as possible in the dirt and mulch; it will be dark in a couple of hours, bettering his chances of getting home undetected.

Inside, Kopf and his Peacemakers search the house, including inside the closet and under the bed of Kim and Ora Lee's bedroom.

"I want you out, Derrick, or I'm calling the police," Kim tells Kopf.

"That would be a waste of time!" Kopf laughs. "The police are tied up with the mobs and riots downtown. They count on me, and people like me, to keep the rest of this great country from fallin' apart. I'm merely performin' my civic duty in order to protect those who are already here, and have been here. That includes you, Kimberly. You're a fine white woman, lap-licker or no. But that chink wife of yours, we don't need another one of them runnin' around."

"You're not the law," Kim says, defiantly. "You're a vigilante, a wannabe-cop, focused on bogus laws the real authorities don't care about enough to bother with. You're a racist and homophobic woman-hater. And your kind is not welcome in this house."

Kopf steps forward. Kim shuts her eyes and prepares to be struck. But Kopf has restraint, and does not raise his arms.

"I'll take your comments under advisement," he says with a professional smile. "Please don't hesitate to bring your concerns to me in the future." He turns and walks down the hall. "Everybody out!" he calls. The Peacemakers leave in single file, and soon Kim is alone again.

THE MOISTURE FROM THE GROUND seeps through to Tucker's knees, blood from his shin is soaking his sock, and on his head tickle strands of a spider web, irritating his skin, but he dares not move. Until the sun sets, he hopes to lay low.

Somebody approaches from the back. Tucker can't see who it is from where he crouches, but as the footsteps get closer, White comes into view. He stops only a few feet away, between Tucker and a large oak.

Pistol in hand, his arms hang limp at his side. From this angle, Tucker is exposed, and if Mr. White turns around, he's a goner. As motionless as possible, he holds his breath.

White is barely hidden behind the tree. He looks back and forth, surveying what he can. Tucker hears more footsteps crunching leaves, a little more distant this time but gradually getting closer. White hears them too, and grins when he sees who it is.

White lifts his pistol and points, but to see at what, Tucker needs to crane his neck. The target is Mr. Harris. Mr. Harris isn't far away, and he carries a pistol as well, but with White obscured by the oak, he is oblivious to the danger.

Tucker is fighting for his would-be family, for the baby who might be named after him, and for the world the baby will grow up in. He springs from the ground, and in two steps, body-checks White into the tree. Caught off guard, White drops the pistol and turns to recognize his attacker. With both palms, Tucker shoves him against the tree – without the gun, White seems to shrink – and hits him again before he falls. Tucker kicks him in the ribs several times while furiously trying but failing to spot the gun among the leaves. He turns to run, but now, it's Mr. Harris who is facing him with a gun.

The gun shakes in Harris's hand. On the ground behind him, White groans in pain. Suddenly there is a banging and rattling; Kim is pounding on the window and yelling.

Mr. Harris's eyes dart back and forth between the two. Tucker turns around to kick White twice more.

"Watch your back in this crowd," Tucker says as he runs past Mr. Harris and through the neighboring backyards in search of a safe passageway across the street.

Mr. Harris watches Tucker disappear around the corner before turning his gaze to the moaning Mr. White. White goes silent as the two men make eye contact. Seeing Mr. Harris towering above him with a gun, White, lying defenselessly on the ground, wets himself.

Mr. Harris tosses his pistol over his shoulder and steps forward.

"I'm not getting my boy back, am I?" he says, stepping forward.

White braces himself for contact, but when there is no assault, he gains confidence and jeers, "I wouldn't count on it."

Head down, Mr. Harris privately quits the Peacemakers and makes his way home.

White makes sure he's out of sight before rolling over and getting up. He is embarrassed and angry about his wet pants, but looking at the ground, he is pleased to discover that he hadn't been lying on a root, a pine cone, or a rock, but on his pistol. He glances at the window, but Kim is no longer there; she has gone to call Ora Lee to urge her not to come home tonight.

He picks up his weapon and, bruised, limps across the street to crouch around the corner of Tucker's house.

THE SUN IS SETTING. Derrick Kopf is home and has finished eating dinner. He may have gone too far breaking into the Blaylock home. It's a gray area. He regrets this, but he will not apologize – a sign of weakness – nor does he intend to admit that he was wrong. Still, some sort of damage control will be needed.

The front windows of his house are open and he hears a gunshot. For all the excitement this evening, there hadn't been a shot fired until now.

Beyond the outskirts of Tucker's lawn, among the painted lines on the pavement, Kopf finds White on the verge of freaking out – mouth open, pale-faced, frightened.

"I, I," he stammers, "he just jumped out of nowhere. I didn't mean to do it. Honest. I mean, it wasn't even me. Someone shot him. Someone else. Not me."

"No, White," Kopf says, in a soothing and comforting voice. "*You* shot him."

"No, no," he babbles, "we can blame it on the cunts across the street. We can say he tried to rape them."

"No, White," Kopf repeats. "*You* shot him. This man was a criminal. He was an animal and you did what you had to do to protect your country. You shot him. And you will be rewarded." Kopf puts a hand on White's shoulder. "*You* shot him."

White swallows. "I shot him."

"You did a good job," Kopf says. "Now, let's get you home." He puts his arm around his minion's shoulder and escorts him away. It's a mess, but Kopf can clean it up.

THE HARRISES HAVE MOVED. Tucker's house across the street is vacant and for sale. And with White in jail, his house may soon be on the market as well. Peacemaker Kopf seems to have influence over whom the houses are sold to, which dulls any glimmer of hope someone might have. Soon a realtor will be here to meet with the Blaylocks, as they too wish to leave.

Kim and Ora Lee sit, each with child, looking out at their once beloved neighborhood. The new laws passed within a week, but the deeds were done in time; both babies will be legal. And if one of the babies is a boy, he will be named Tucker.

FRIEND REQUEST

CLAY SENT ME A FRIEND REQUEST with a message. It said nothing special; he was wondering what I'd been up to all this time. I hadn't thought of Clay in years and hadn't seen him in even longer. As children, we lived on the same street. Back then, we didn't need a better reason to be friends.

If childhood ends with puberty, we were knocking on the door. Matt, Tobin, and I had just lost our best friend after his family moved to the rich side of the city. We were still in mourning when the new kid arrived. This put Clay at a disadvantage from the start. Clay never fared well in comparison to others.

He certainly didn't make a strong first impression. Clay was smaller than Matt, Tobin, and me. He spoke with saliva and he laughed inward, as if it didn't come natural, like he didn't actually think something was funny and he was just trying to fit in. He was an odd little runt. And we couldn't make sense of his Jacksonville Jaguars clothes. They don't like the Jaguars even in Jacksonville, so why was a kid in upstate New York telling people he rooted for an expansion team?

Clay's mom and Lyle lived together even though they weren't married. That was unusual. My parents had recently separated, but at least they used to be married. And Clay called him Lyle, not Dad. Maybe Lyle wasn't Clay's real dad. I never learned for sure.

Lyle yelled. Nobody had air conditioning, so windows were always open during the summer. Tobin lived next door to Clay, and from inside Tobin's house we could hear Lyle screaming at Clay. Sometimes we heard a bang or a crash. After those outbursts, his mother answered the door to tell us Clay couldn't come out to play. Come September, Clay missed time at school.

We were not destined to be lifelong friends, Clay and I, though for a while I ran into him here and there. He made the news when he was a high school senior. After school one afternoon, he and a friend were racing to Burger King. Burger King was at the bottom of a hill down a stretch of road where everyone had gotten a speeding ticket at least once. The road narrowed from four lanes to two, which was good news for Clay because he was winning. But the cars in front were slowing down, and for Clay, slowing down meant risking the lead. There wasn't any oncoming traffic, and, because he couldn't imagine anything worse than pulling in last to Burger King, he changed lanes to pass the slow pokes. The reason for the slowing, however, was that at the front of the line an elderly woman was about to pull into her driveway. She turned left just as Clay tried to pass. Clay, who was wearing a seatbelt, suffered only minor injuries when he slammed into the driver's side of the turning car. The woman didn't make it. Clay was eighteen, and he did some time.

IN THE MORNINGS, Matt, Tobin, Clay, and I would bid our parents farewell until supper and race out of our neighborhood, across the expressway on-ramp, over cars screaming and eighteen-wheelers roaring underneath the bridge, with a quick stop at the gas station to buy pop and slushies, and down the boulevard a ways before finally veering off to the right into a labyrinth of dirt bike trails. The trails were well-worn and mostly easy to navigate, though in one spot a log had fallen, leaving only a ten-inch gap to thread bike tires through. But we were so practiced that only occasionally would anyone wipe out.

A mile in any direction we might've been run over by a minivan, but the woods felt like wilderness. There were even fish in the creek. I never saw one more than a couple of inches long, but we tried hooking them anyway. Away from the water there were hills that were great fun to bike down, especially after some bigger kids piled up a dirt mound at the bottom where, going full speed, we could get serious air. And in the winter, the four of us simultaneously raced down on sleds. The objective was to create the greatest sledding collision ever. If someone made it to the bottom of the hill unscathed, he would look back at the mess of sleds, snow, and limbs, and feel sorry for himself.

Unless someone's parent happened to be going for a run through the woods, we went hours without adult contact. Nobody was ever kidnapped. We swore with the best of them, but we never did drugs or smoked cigarettes. Pretty much everyone suffered bloody noses, bruised ribs, and mild concussions, but nobody died.

What we needed Clay for most was two-on-two football. With only three people, we were limited to Murder the Man With the Ball, which was fun, but not the real thing. Nobody wanted to be paired with Clay, but Matt, Tobin, and I used a steady and tactless rotation to decide who was stuck with him on any given day.

It was hard having Clay as the only option. Matt, Tobin, and I were pretty evenly matched — I can't say one of us was better than the other two — but Clay couldn't catch or throw. He could hand off to someone all right, but handing off to him proved more interesting.

"Okay, Clay, you're going to line up in the backfield to my left. I'll yell 'Hut!' and you go in motion, cross over to the right. Then it's 'Hut! Hike!' and I'll pitch the ball to you. You're the Jaguars' running back, all right? What's his name?" Clay looked at me blankly. "Never mind. Anyway, they'll be following you, so cut back toward me immediately. I'll block the way and you take it in. Ready?"

We broke the huddle, and I held the ball out to where I best guessed the line of scrimmage to be. Matt was in front of me, ready to count five Mississippi before he could blitz. Clay lined up to my left but in front of the ball – off sides.

Tobin was lined up opposite Clay. "I think you gotta back up," Tobin said.

Clay took a step back.

"More," I said.

Clay took another step back.

"Back up like ten feet, man," I said.

Clay was a deer in headlights, so I called "time out" to go over the instructions again. This time I pointed right at the spot I wanted him to stand, and to the route I wanted him to run, not worried about giving our game plan away to the defense. He seemed to get it, so I took my position back at the line.

"Hut!" I yelled. Clay didn't move. "That's your cue, dude," I said. Clay jogged to his right, behind me. "Hut! Hike!"

I lateraled the ball back toward Clay. He held out his arms, but the ball hit him in the face.

"Fumble!" Tobin yelled.

A loose ball meant Matt and Tobin didn't need to wait for five Mississippi before crossing the line. Matt was the first to the ball and bent over to pick it up and take it the distance, but his feet got in the way and he booted the ball out of reach.

"Jump on it, Clay!" I yelled, breaking after the ball behind Matt and Tobin. Clay was quick and had a beat on it. He lunged, but his aim was off and the ball squirted inches away. I put my arms up and took out Tobin. It might've been an illegal hit, but we were both laughing before we hit the ground.

With Clay on his belly, Matt tried to jump over him to get to the ball, but Clay rose just as Matt was midflight and tripped him. Matt fell on his face while Clay yelped in pain. Tobin and I rose to catch up with them. Clay army-crawled to the ball and got a hand on it just as Matt arrived. Tobin dove through the air, landed on the two bodies, kneeing them both in the back, and pronounced, "I got it!" Not wanting to be left out of the pile-up, I jumped on top.

When we got the ball back, I made Clay quarterback. I didn't mind taking handoffs, but it got boring, so I told him to throw it up. He had no aim, but if he got the ball high enough, I thought I'd have a decent chance of making a play. The first attempt was remarkably successful, which I guess gave us false hope, because Clay's next two throws somehow went backwards. Tobin pointed out that an incomplete backward pass was the same as a fumble. I decided not to risk having Clay throw backwards again. I took over at quarterback and stuck the ball square in Clay's gut. It took him a second to secure the ball, long enough for Matt to meet him in the backfield and take his knees out. We had to punt.

I stuck with the conservative game plan each

time we had the ball. Occasionally Clay would wriggle away and picked up a couple of yards. Then we'd slap fives as if we'd just won the Super Bowl. More often than not, though, either Matt or Tobin would barrel into his chest and drill him into the ground. One time, Clay tried an ill-advised leap into the air, as if he could fly over his would-be tacklers. Matt caught him and, with both Clay and the ball in his arms, ran the length of the field for a safety. Tobin brought to our attention the "forward progress" rule, which prevented such defensive plays, but I let the safety stand anyway.

This went on for a good half hour in Tobin's and Clay's backyards. Clay never complained. He took hand-off after hand-off, and big hit after big hit. When he didn't rise right away, I held out my hand to pull him up. He seemed to like that, and he smiled. Then I gave him the hand-off, and he got leveled again. The score was as lopsided as ever, but it sure was hilarious.

Clay was tackled for roughly the thousandth time that afternoon when we heard Lyle crash through the backdoor of their house.

"Get off of him!" he yelled, instantly upon us.

When Lyle said something, we listened. His tone of voice was familiar, except we were used to hearing it from a distance. Matt, Tobin, and I backed away, eager to avoid a beating.

"I don't like the way you're playing!" Lyle said.

"It's okay, it's okay," Clay insisted.

"It's not okay!" Lyle glared at us. "You're just hitting him over and over. Some friends you are!"

He grabbed Clay by the arm and pulled him toward the house. Clay moved his feet as fast as he could to keep from dragging. "Ow," Clay referred to Lyle's grip on his arm. "Ow ow ow!" he cried.

I THINK CLAY IS DOING OKAY NOW. I'm not sure if he ever finished high school, but he got out of jail and got a job at one of those instant oil change joints. Before I moved away, I saw him there every three thousand miles. We never were able to mold him into the friend we wanted him to be. Still, he was happy to see me and spoke fondly of the good old days. He wished we were kids again. He used to ask about Matt and Tobin, but those guys haven't kept in touch. I never asked him about Lyle, though it was never far from the tip of my tongue.

WHILE WE PLAYED FOOTBALL in our backyards, there was more to do in the woods. We built fires but quickly put them out before a grownup could get us in trouble. We waded in the creek and caught crayfish in a bucket. We fished for hours without hooking anything but weeds. After rain, we went down mud slides climaxing into the deepest parts of the creek.

We rode our bikes a lot. Sometimes we took the straightest and most direct path, so we could build up the most speed, but sometimes we went out of our way in search of obstacles, which was slower but more challenging. Either way, we always ended up flying down the big dirt hills, slamming the brakes at the bottom so hard that the back tire spun us around and we finished facing the other direction.

Clay wasn't that stable on a bike. He was able to build up a good pace on the paved streets in our neighborhood, but he didn't come close to the same speeds in the woods, where he was convinced the trees, logs, and bends were out to get him. Eventually he built enough courage to go down the big hills, but never before coming to a complete stop at the edge, and then inching forward with his feet on the ground until he couldn't control it anymore and rolled the rest of the way down, pumping the hand brakes as he went. At the bottom, he'd coast off to the side, and, before coming back up top to join us, pause to catch his breath and calm his thumping heart.

The speed bump at the bottom of the hill turned up randomly one day and instantly added another dimension to our shenanigans. I was already going a healthy speed around the bend before even getting to the top of the decline, and by the time I got to the bottom I was going so fast that the wind in my face almost stung. I hit the bump and leaned back, and the bike and I catapulted high into the air before bouncing back to earth. After that, it was a wobbly and mildly terrifying twenty feet before I regained control and avoided the patch of trees that were inconveniently too close. Then we all raced back to the paths to build up speed and do it again.

Tobin was the first to lose control. His aim was off, and he went over the speed bump too far to the left, where it was uneven. The bike tipped over midair and crashed to the ground on its side. Pinned between the bike and the ground, Tobin slid for several feet before flipping the bike off and hopping up.

"Wow!" he exclaimed. The rough dirt had scraped a good bit of skin off of his legs just below the knee, and there was already blood, visible even from the top of the hill. "Man, that hurt!" he said, clearly in pain, but relishing it. He got back on his bike, howled briefly as he pedaled back up top, where he bypassed my turn in line, sped down the hill and over the bump, picked up some air, and skidded to a stop a few feet in front of a large tree.

"That was your best one yet!" I called down to him.

"All right, killer," Matt said to Clay. "You're up."

Clay stood with Matt and me at the top and peered down the hill toward the bottom, where a little mound of dirt, a mountain to him, stood in his way.

"I don't know, guys," he said, with tiny saliva bubbles collecting at the corners of his mouth. "It's a little scary looking."

"It's not scary," Matt said, rolling his eyes.

"You don't have to do it," I said. "But we've all

done it like twenty times already. It's easy."

"You just saw me fall," Tobin said, "and I'm fine." Clay glanced warily at Tobin's bloody leg. "It doesn't even hurt," Tobin insisted.

"Just do it," Matt said. "Or else you're a baby."

"It's fine, man," I said. "Go for it. It feels really cool."

Clay looked down the hill again, and then back at us. He sat on his bike and, with his toes still touching the ground, inched forward, as if to the edge of a sky-scraper.

"All right!" Matt said. "Now we have a show!"

And Clay pushed off! It was one of his more daring trips down the hill. He didn't even try to slow down with his feet, and if he was pumping the hand brakes, I couldn't tell. It was the most confident I'd ever seen him, or would ever see him again. He looked like he was having fun, like he felt good about himself, as if he fit in.

He may not have been pumping the brakes downhill, but once he reached the bottom, he slammed them hard. His body's momentum pushed him forward and he leaned over the handlebars. The front tire wedged with the bumpy little ramp and jammed the bike, and inertia sent Clay through the air and crash-landing shoulder first into the ground.

His screams were heard throughout the woods. Matt, Tobin, and I were down the hill in seconds. Tobin grabbed hold of Clay's arm to help him off the ground, but Clay's shrieks only grew louder.

"I'll go get help!" Tobin said with an air of responsibility. He tore off on his bike and out of sight. He couldn't have been gone more than ninety seconds before Matt and I started wondering what was taking so long.

Clay had a broken collarbone, we would later learn. Matt and I did what we could to console him. We told him that Tobin would be back soon with his parents. We told him a doctor would set everything right. We apologized for making him go down the hill. We told him how brave he'd been, and how good he looked as he approached the bottom. It didn't matter what we said, the sobs, tears, and mucus kept coming.

Matt couldn't take it any longer and made up some crap about how Tobin must've gotten lost.

"Can you walk?" I asked Clay once Matt had disappeared.

Clay nodded silently and got his feet under him to stand up. I balanced our two bikes on either side of me and, with one hand on each set of handlebars, slowly rolled them up the hill. The pedals banged and scraped against my shins. We walked for ten minutes, Clay's whimpering and sniffling my only clues to his presence, before we and the bikes emerged from the woods onto the sidewalk along the four lanes.

A familiar car screeched as it pulled to a stop at the side of the road.

"Oh my God, Clay, honey," Clay's mother said as she got out of the car and rushed to her son's side. Clay's crying had subsided, but he let loose again in his mother's bosom.

Tobin got out of the car, too, and stood sheepishly by my side. Lyle had driven. He popped the trunk and picked up my bike.

"That's mine," I said.

He put it back down, glared at me, picked up the other bike, and threw it in the trunk. Clay's mom helped her son into the back seat of the car and buckled the seatbelt for him.

"See you later, Clay," I said.

The grown-ups got into the car without saying anything to me. Clay didn't look up from the back seat. Lyle glared at us violently once more before pulling away from the curb, into traffic, and down the road. I still had my bike as Tobin and I began walking home. It was rush hour, and the road was loud with speeding cars inches from the sidewalk.

"You all right?" I said to Tobin. He'd been silent since he returned with Clay's parents. His lips moved, but I couldn't make out any words.

Lyle hadn't said a word, but the look he'd given us more than made up for it. I remembered him scolding us once before, and I was sure Tobin was thinking, too: some friends we are.

Friend Request

BEFRIENDING THE SCUM
OF THE EARTH

I BELIEVE IN FORGIVENESS. I want to give people the benefit of the doubt. In theory, I believe in rehabilitation. I do not, however, want to be friends with a pedophile.

Vince bought the house between the nuns and me. On moving day, the neighborhood residents formed a receiving line, and Vince shook hands with each of the parents from across the street, the middle-aged divorcées, the nuns, and the Elder Statesman. The Elder Statesman gathered everyone and gave a speech, not only to offer Vince his gracious hospitality, but also to speak of the long-standing tradition of high character and moral fiber exuded by the residents of his beloved street.

Perhaps Vince should simply have taken advantage of the gathering to make one announcement and get it over with. Instead, he shook everybody's hand, told jokes, laughed at theirs, and accepted fruit baskets and plates of brownies. Not until the following week did he go door-to-door to inform everybody of his record.

I was slow to react, having had zero prior experience listening to a man tell me he'd been found guilty of diddling little boys. When he finished his court-mandated speech, he stuck out his hand. I hesitated, as if his arms and hands were covered in slime or crawling with parasites. But I resisted the urge to back away, and, because social convention says so, I shook it. "Welcome to the neighborhood," I said.

Compared to the reaction of the rest of the neighborhood, I might as well have said, "You and I are going to be best friends."

At first, I was one with the neighborhood. Neighbors complained to me as much as to anyone. "There ought to be a law." "How can someone like that be allowed back into civilized society?" "We should send them all to an island where they can rape each other to death." "If nothing else, we need to pray for him." That last was from one of the nuns. The nuns and I were showered with pity for having to live on either side of the offender.

The Elder Statesman had inherited his home when his own parents died thirty years earlier, decades after he was born in that same house, in the same bedroom he slept in now. He polled interest in a neighborhood meeting to discuss how to oust Vince from the zip code, but the general feeling was that nothing legal could be done. And, because of the moral fiber of the neighborhood's residents, nothing *illegal* was even suggested.

I happened to be on my porch, reading, when Timmy lost control of his soccer ball and it bounced into Vince's front yard. Vince wasn't outside; I don't think he was even home. Timmy ran across the street to retrieve his ball. From inside the house, his mother glanced out the window and screamed at the top of her lungs, "Timmy, get out of that yard right now! Timmy, do you hear me?! Come inside! Now!!!"

In less than a week, Timmy's house was on the market. The family moved not long after, before the house was even sold.

Our only other family couldn't risk taking on a second mortgage. They installed a full-perimeter fence instead.

"I'm grilling burgers," Vince said to me on Saturday. I was still half-asleep and didn't have a shirt on. "Come on over!"

"Uh, okay."

In his backyard the charcoal grill was already fired up. He threw on two patties as I walked through the gate. He gave me the choice of several cheeses, recommending the Gruyere. I sat in front of one of two placemats set on his new patio furniture. I was either the only person invited or the only one who had accepted. Also on the table was every condiment I'd ever heard of and a half-dozen flavors of Lays potato chips.

I loaded up and took a bite. With blood dripping down my chin, I gave the chef my compliments.

I spotted the nuns sitting in their sun porch next door. I waved, and after several seconds, one of them reluctantly waved back. Mrs. Hafenrichter, my next-door neighbor in the other direction, stepped outside to refill her bird feeder. She glared. For a moment, I felt bad for Vince before I realized she was glaring at *me*.

Around this time in my life, Maria and I had an awkward but ultimately pleasant conversation in which we agreed to date each other exclusively. This was exciting, since she was my first serious girlfriend since my ex-fiancée had ended our relationship a while back following our miscarriage. Suddenly, Maria was coming over several times a week. It was inevitable that she and Vince would meet.

"This is a heck of a spread, Vincenzo," I remember saying. When he had suggested we come over to watch the playoff game and "get something to eat," I had assumed he meant ordering a pizza. But, no, his entire dining room table was filled with sandwiches, salsa, queso, chips, veggies, microbrews, and cocktail wieners.

"Thanks for having us," Maria said, giving him a half-hug and kissing him on the cheek.

"Is anyone else coming?" I asked.

Nobody else was coming.

Later, when I was home alone, I googled him. He'd been accused and found guilty of molesting two boys, brothers age six and eight. He adamantly denied the charges throughout the trial and into his incarceration. Actually seeing this in print made my heart flutter. He looked horrible in the pictures, too, as twisted as the descriptions made him out to be, like a real-life monster. But he did his time and was even released early. Not long after, those same two brothers were in the news again. This time, though, it was their father who was found guilty of molestation and sent to jail.

VINCE TALKED ME INTO going out to lunch one day. He came to pick me up from work, but he was early, and I had a few things to finish up, so he sat nearby hobnobbing with my co-worker, really hitting it off. Then my co-worker's wife and four-year-old son arrived for his lunch. Vince stopped joking long enough to say, "Ma'am, when knowingly in the vicinity of a child, I am legally obligated to inform you that..." It was downhill from there.

When I got back to work after lunch, my boss approached me. "I'm sorry, I didn't realize it was Bring a Pervert to Work Day. Did y'all realize it's Bring a Pervert to Work Day? If I'd known it was Bring a Pervert to Work Day, I would've gone over to the penitentiary and picked me up a pervert so he could mingle with these fine people and their families. But I didn't know! Why didn't somebody tell me it was Bring a Pervert to Work Day?"

It took some doing, but I was finally able to convince him that it was not Bring a Pervert to Work Day.

"Don't you be bringing a pervert here, man. I don't want no perverts in this office. Nobody else wants no perverts in this office. You want to hang out with perverts, you do it on your own time. But keep your pervert away from here."

Ever since, people have been keeping their distance.

I COME HOME, and Vince is outside, and he waves hello, so I wave back, but I'm really thinking, "go away, man, you disgust me." He calls for me to come over, but it's windy, the leaves are rustling, and a car drives by, so I pretend not to hear him, and I go inside.

But he comes over and suggests we "watch a movie or something", so I tell him I have plans and have to get ready to leave. I don't actually have plans, though, and Maria is busy, so I go to Barnes & Noble and read until it's time to go to bed.

But Maria likes Vince, and she invites Kristen over to meet him. Kristen likes him too, and next thing I know, the three of them rope me into double dates. Vince makes elaborate three-course meals, spending entire days on prep work. He refuses Kristen's and Maria's help, but unofficially appoints me *sous* chef. Sometimes he makes name cards, so we don't sit at the same places every week: men on one side, women on the other; Maria and me on one side, Vince and Kristen on the other; or pairing himself with Maria, and me with Kristen.

In the living room, we sit around and play games, talking late into the evening, until Kristen and Vince hint that they're ready to be alone, leaving Maria and me to walk the twenty feet from Vince's front door to mine.

The Elder Statesman knocks on my door and invites himself in. Along with the rest of the neighborhood, he is concerned with my budding friendship with Vince, when "What we want to do is make him feel unwanted. We want to be hostile. We want to drive him away."

The Elder Statesman is a nice man, but with his long white beard he resembles an ancient Greek philosopher, and I feel inferior in his presence.

"I don't know," I mumble. "I try to treat others the way I'd like to be treated."

"That's admirable, son, and you have fine character. But a monster should be treated like a monster."

"But he's a nice guy, if you get to know him."

"No, son, he's not a nice guy. He's the lowest of the low. Less than dirt. I hate to think of what he's doing to that poor girl he's brainwashed into coming over all the time. Please don't trap yourself into defending the scum of the earth."

"But he didn't do it. It was the father. Vince was framed; I'm sure of it. He always denied it. But he did the time, and now the father is doing his."

"Is that what he's been feeding you? You're a good boy, son, but you're naïve, and I'm sorry you fell for his tricks."

"But it's in the papers."

In truth, Vince has never once talked about it, and I sure never brought it up. Even when he went door-to-door when he first moved in, instead of saying "I'm a child molester," he said, "I was accused and found guilty of —" which is not actually a confession. And if little boys really do turn him on, what's he doing with Kristin all the time? I generally have faith in the legal system, but if what they say is true, then I am friends with a pervert.

I hear Maria pull up to the curb, but several minutes pass and she still hasn't come inside. I go outside to investigate, and I see her two doors down, out of earshot, having what looks like a serious conversation with the nuns. One of the nuns notices me first. Then Maria turns around, wide-eyed and in shock.

"Is Vince a pedophile?" she demands. She won't come inside, and the nuns are watching. "They said he raped all these kids and went to prison for it. They said there was a family across the street that moved away because he was preying on their children."

"Vince never touched the kids across the

street."

"But you knew and didn't tell me?"

I put my head down and stare at the ground. Lying never does any good.

"I knew, yes."

"And you let me go inside his house?"

I shrug and softly nod.

"You let me hug him? Kiss him on the cheek? You left the two of us alone in the same room?"

"It was little boys, not grown women," I mumble.

"Ew! Gross!" She shudders. "You're his friend!" she accuses. "Why wouldn't you tell me? You even let me set him up with Kristen. Oh my God, Kristen!"

She backs away from me as if I'm infected by pedophilia by association. She rushes for her car, dialing Kristen as she goes. I know this will be the end of Vince and Kristen. And a phone call the next day finishes off Maria and me.

"Maria left me," I tell Vince.

"I too am single again," Vince replies matter-of-factly.

I buy the beer, he the rib-eyes, and we console each other.

"Did I ever tell you I was engaged?" I say to Vince.

"No, I didn't know that. What happened?"

"It shouldn't've happened, really. This was a few years ago. We started dating in college, and after graduation she got a job down here and moved. We kept it going, long-distance, but to be honest, it wasn't going that well. But then she got pregnant, so we decided to get married. I got a job down here real easily, and we made an offer on a house. But then she miscarried. Everything happened so fast. She was twelve weeks in, maybe only ten. So we decided there was no need to rush into marriage anymore. But I'd already started my new job, and I liked the house, so even though she broke up with me pretty soon after that, I bought this house anyway."

Vince puts a hand on my shoulder, caresses it with his pinky, and squeezes. "Sorry to hear that."

"I still like this house, " I say. "And I like this neighborhood. I plan on staying here for a long time. I'm glad you moved in."

"You're a good friend," he agrees.

"So that's my story," I say. "What about you? Do you have any long-ago tales of sorrow and woe? Any deep dark secrets?"

This is as blunt as I can be. He stares off into the distance, as if he's thinking really hard, before turning to me with a smile. "Can't say that I do," he says. "Life's been okay to me."

"Huh," I say.

That's it. We finish our steaks. Later, I go home.

LAST CARESS

A PAIR OF SUICIDES has so shaken Jordy's life that his nephew's moving in registers only as a blip. A state trooper picked up the kid trying to hitchhike on the interstate. Jordy was perplexed that he got the call, but relieved for the distraction. At the station, his nephew amuses him by calling him "Dad", so Jordy returns with "Son."

The kid doesn't know much, but he's aware that his grandparents, the snowbirds, have left for Florida and that Jordy is housesitting. Running away didn't pan out, so the new and quite frankly better plan is to live with his bachelor uncle, the rock star.

"Hello, my darling," Bethany jokes when they walk in. "How did it go at the station?"

"Huh?" the kid says. Whoever this woman is, she is not part of the kid's plan. He asks his uncle, "Did you get married?"

His uncle doesn't answer, but the woman thinks it's funny. The kid doesn't know her, but he hopes she'll leave soon so he and his uncle can be manly, eat chicken wings, and watch bloody movies. But across the house, he hears a baby cry.

"There's your cousin," Bethany tells him, "fussing again. I'll get him."

The kid stares at his uncle. "Since when do you have a kid?"

ON THE PHONE, Jordy learns about his sister's pending divorce. He agrees to look after her son until she sorts things out. How old is he? Jordy regrets not asking. As he drove to the police station, he pictured an eight-year-old. Now he's thinking teenager.

To his surprise, Bethany knows.

"How do you know?"

"I remember when he was born. I held him in the hospital. You dumped me not long after."

"Right," Jordy recalls. "We were seniors."

"I cried," Bethany says.

"I remember."

"You broke my heart."

"I know."

"You're not sorry."

"I was at the time."

– But sometimes I wish I'd hurt you more.

He doesn't say this out loud. He'd broken up with her, true, but a few months later it felt like he was the one who'd been dumped. Among the feelings she ignites inside him, anger and resentment dominate. For years he fantasized about telling her off. Now he's got to be careful not to drive her away.

Bethany appreciates that Jordy got the raw end of their complicated history, though she makes no apologies for doing what was right for herself. She forces a smile that Jordy doesn't reciprocate.

"It's time for bed," she says, and stands up.

Despite spending much of the year in Florida, Jordy's parents still own the three-bedroom house he grew up in. Bethany sleeps next to the room Jordy is converting into a nursery. Upstairs, the kid has an air mattress in his grandmother's sewing room. Jordy sleeps down the hall from him.

JORDY'S EULOGY is still fresh in the fans' consciousness. He had fled San Francisco, unable to endure the posthumous post-production arguments, leaving Dave to fight, alone and in vain, the legal battles. He, Dave, and Bradley had shared the same vision for the album, Jordy swears. The widow claimed otherwise, and the executives have been siding with her.

"Punk is dead," she claimed. "Punk hasn't been popular in years."

"We're not trying to make a punk album; we're making a ska-reggae album."

"Ska is dead, too!" the widow preached. "Wake

up, guys; it's all been done before. This isn't 1996 anymore. This is your last chance to make something of this band, to leave a mark in the history books, to give Bradley a lasting legacy."

And so the dream is dead. With three unexpected house guests, Jordy has had little time to dwell on this. Some nights, they played for a thousand people, though sometimes, in a small city on a Tuesday, they'd have fewer than two hundred. They earned enough to support themselves, but not so much to afford real luxuries. Jordy was the most straight-edge punk rocker anyone knew, but he'd witnessed Bradley get high literally every day for months at a time. They sat across from each other, co-writing songs, with a joint in Bradley's mouth. More than once Bradley woke up drunk and stayed drunk until the show was over and he could pass out again on the tour bus.

Jordy may have suspected, but he'd never actually known Bradley to take anything harder than weed until he'd walked in on him lying on the floor, foam and vomit dribbling from his mouth.

Now thirty, Jordy is out of a job and qualified for nothing.

— Brad, you fucker, you selfish prick, you ruined everything. I'm so sorry. Please forgive me.

"YOU TAUGHT ME HOW to unhook a bra." It's true, she admits. "And you taught me well. Now, girls are always impressed with how quickly I get it un-done."

"Don't tell me that!" Bethany smacks him in the chest.

They are ten years younger, lying on Jordy's twin bed, facing each other, posters on the wall, empty cans of Mountain Dew on the floor. Two classes in the morning and band practice that evening, Jordy's after-noon is for Bethany. His parents are at work and they have the house to themselves. They will remain fully-clothed, but his hands are on her waist, under her shirt, and he's already unhooked her bra.

"I never should've let you under my shirt," she says, referencing the past, pretending not to notice them currently. "I regret that."

"As long as you accept responsibility."

"Me? You took something from me."

He'd never touched breasts before. Bethany gave him the green light for his eighteenth birthday. He didn't ask permission, Jordy would point out in later arguments, nor could he even bring himself to do it; he shook with fear and had to fight back tears. A week later, Bethany encouraged him again, and this time he followed through. After that, the floodgates were open. Bethany didn't mind until they broke up.

"I didn't take anything from you," Jordy ar-gues. On his twin bed, he maneuvers Bethany onto her back and rolls on top of her, his hands sliding up her sides. "You're still a virgin. And besides, you've gone further with other dudes."

Bethany's least proud decision, she'd gotten involved with a guy who, recognizing how important the church was to her, said he was a Jehovah's Witness, guessing incorrectly that Jehovah's Witnesses comprised a sect of Protestantism, like the Lutherans and Methodists. He was lying to get in her pants, and she fell for it.

"You told everyone that after you and I broke up you weren't going to date for an entire year to focus on God. You said that *while* we were going out; how fucked up is that? And then you went out with a Jehovah's Witness."

"Don't throw that back at me!" Bethany defends herself but otherwise ignores his profanity.

She pushes Jordy, and he lets himself be tipped over. Now, Bethany is on top, straddling him as if on horseback, pressing her palms against the Suicide Machines logo on the chest of his shirt.

"That was a gigantic mistake, and I regret everything about him. But I never gave him my heart. I only ever gave it to you."

Twice, Bethany told Jordy that she couldn't see or talk to him *ever again*, the first time because Jordy was too big of a distraction during her year of intimacy with the Lord. The designated year had been over for months when Bethany eventually called off the ban. Except for the Jehovah's Witness, Bethany had successfully kept her vow to kiss dating goodbye. Now she was in a courtship – group outings only – with her husband-to-be, dead set on becoming a pastor's wife. But the pastor-in-training sensed a strain, spiritually, so Bethany faced her fears and reconnected with Jordy to sever their still-intact soul-tie.

As they prayed, she felt the hands of God undo the soul-tie. Without the soul-tie, Bethany said, they might as well be friends again. Like old times, they began calling each other freely, and only semi-discreetly; Bethany's parents gave her an earful every time they answered one of Jordy's calls. When they were together, alone in his house in his bedroom on his bed, their chemistry got the better of them. She permitted his grabby hands over much of her body and, while their lips never touched, he spent significant time kissing her neck and ears.

Unlike Bethany, Jordy had not felt God's presence. Because she'd turned into a spiritual whacko, Jordy's interest in actually going out with her had disappeared, but he was so stoked to have her back in his life that he played along.

HAVING HIS NEPHEW HERE isn't as much fun as Jordy thought it would be. Maybe it's because of the baby, or Bethany's fault, but the kid spends most of his time in his room blasting music. Jordy would complain, but the kid has great taste; every now and then he hears Bradley's sweet voice seeping through the walls.

"Hey!" Jordy pounds. "Open the damn door! Why didn't you tell me you were supposed to be in school all week?"

"I'm thirteen," the kid replies. "Of course I'm supposed to be in school."

"You don't think you could've mentioned that? Your mother calls me up, super pissed that I'm letting you ditch every day. How about helping me out a little instead of treating me like a chump. Starting Monday, I'm driving you to school."

He stomps down the stairs, upset at being taken advantage of. Bethany is eavesdropping in the living room while the baby fusses angrily in his crib.

"Are you just going to sit on your ass?" Jordy asks, gesturing toward the nursery. "Or are you going to take care of that?"

Without a word, Bethany gets up to change the baby's diaper.

"WHEN'S THE LAST TIME you went to church?" Bethany asks now. They are sitting together on the couch, not on opposite ends, but not touching either.

"You judging me?"

"Just asking. Do you ever think about going again?"

"I went the Sunday before you got here." At the end of his street is a Presbyterian church with a 10:30 service, convenient for both its time and location. "I don't know how long before that. Even Brad's funeral wasn't in a church."

"Do you still believe in God?"

In high school, Jordy played in a Christian punk band. Before the last song of every set, the front man, Michael, shared his beliefs with the audience and invited anyone with questions about God to come talk to someone in the band. This made Jordy uncomfortable – he had little confidence in his ability to have a serious theological discussion – but to his relief, he was never approached.

The strength of Jordy's faith fluctuated, at times borderline-agnostic, but he'd never stopped believing altogether. His chosen career field, however, was openly anti-Christian, anti-religion in general. But Jordy was always an introvert, and in the punk community, only Dave and Bradley knew that he'd once been a regular church-goer. As atheism grew in popularity, and Bad Religion, NOFX, and Anti-Flag were all ripping Jesus a new one, Bradley refrained from writing anti-God lyrics, out of respect for Jordy, and instead wrote about political and social issues, drug use, and sex, including one reggae song so dirty Bradley sang half of it in Spanish.

"DOES HE KNOW I've seen your boobies?" Jordy remembers asking Bethany.

He, Bradley, and Dave have three shows lined up for the weekend, and they're entering the recording studio next week for the first time. Otherwise he would consider cancelling band practice to spend the rest of the day with her.

"God is omniscient, so, yes."

"Not God; your boyfriend."

"No, he doesn't," she says. "And stop saying 'boobies'; you sound like a twelve-year-old."

"If you're actually going to marry him, don't you think your husband-to-be should know that I've seen your boobies and that the Jehovah's Witness touched your pussy?"

He disregards the pious façade everyone else has bought. In their love triangle, Jordy is the bad guy, and sometimes he plays it up. They used to watch racy movies and listen to the same punk bands. On days he feels especially antagonistic, he tells her he doesn't understand what she sees in that preppy douchebag. Bethany will put up with anything from him.

"You're being a jerk," she says. "And he knows about the Jehovah's Witness."

"Why don't you tell him about me?"

"That wouldn't go well. He doesn't like you."

"He likes the Jehovah's Witness?"

"He never met the Jehovah's Witness."

JORDY HAD BEEN WHOLLY DEVOTED to his high school Christian punk band and thought of little else during its sixteen-month run. The summer after high school graduation, Michael dissolved the band. God has other plans for me, he told a devastated Jordy.

Here is Michael now; Jordy sees him pull up and meets him on the driveway. For a while they would run into each other at shows. But – seven years? eight? – Jordy hasn't seen him in a long time.

They shake hands and agree on how good it is to see each other.

"I'm sorry about Bradley," Michael says. "I can't even imagine. I remember talking to him when you guys were first starting out. Seemed like a great guy. I'm here for you if you need an ear."

"Appreciate that."

"What are you going to do now?"

"I don't know. There's a lot of legal bullshit that Dave is trying to sort through. Then, maybe he and I will start a new band. I dread starting over, though. You playing with anyone these days? I always thought you were the best guitarist I ever played with. Maybe even better than Brad."

"That's high praise! And I always thought of you as the best drummer I ever played with. Time's proven me right."

They smile, remembering the few shows they'd performed in church basements and rec centers thirteen years ago, the excitement they felt after a good rehearsal when they talked about the future.

"Listen," Michael says. "I'm guessing you know why I'm here."

Jordy assumes correctly, though she's out at the moment.

In youth group, because he and Michael were bandmates, Jordy wasn't totally ostracized like some of the total dorks. Still, they rarely spoke outside of band practice; Michael hung with the cool kids while Jordy sat with the rejects. On Sunday mornings Jordy looked longingly at Michael's group, wishing for an invitation. Michael at least said hi. In the same clique was Michael's cousin. Michael's cousin never gave Jordy the time of day. Michael's cousin eventually married Bethany. Now he's sent Michael to do his dirty work for him.

"He needs her home. Their kids are asking hard questions, and he's freaking out. I've never seen him this way. And his parishioners are running out of patience. He might be forced to take a sabbatical."

– Kids?

"I don't care what happens to him."

"Maybe not, but even you have to agree it's wrong to steal another man's wife."

– Even me?

"I stole nothing. She's a grown woman making grown-up decisions; I don't tell her what to do. She came here on her own and she's welcome to stay as long as she wants."

"Come on, we're all friends. Think about it objectively. Do the right thing and send her home."

"Are we friends?" Jordy asks accusingly, stunning Michael. "When was the last time you called me up to see how I was doing, or ask me to dinner? And I remember an awful lot of youth group hangs I wasn't invited to. I haven't heard from you in ten years. You'll get no favors from me."

Michael hasn't done right by Jordy, siding with his cousin without attempting to understand the other side. Few things in life are black and white, and Jordy is broken. But why? He's travelled the world. Thousands of fans have sung their songs at concerts. He and Michael? They weren't anything. They played eleven shows total.

"I'm sorry, Jordy," Michael says, humbled and sympathetic. "I had no idea you felt this way. Let's have dinner sometime, unrelated to this. And we can just talk, all right?"

"If you want."

"I'll call you," Michael says. "I promise."

Jordy reluctantly accepts a handshake before Michael turns for his car parked on the street and drives away. The house is silent, so the baby must either be happy or asleep. Or maybe Bethany took him with her; Jordy doesn't know. His feet remain firmly planted on the driveway until Bethany gets back and pulls in.

"Michael was just here," he tells her. "You know, your cousin-in-law."

"Oh!" she says, taken aback. "What did he want?"

"How many kids do you have?"

"Three. What did Michael want?"

"For you to go back to the parsonage and pretend it's 1950 again."

"And what did you say?"

"I told him we're fucking."

"You did not!"

"No, I didn't." Jordy looks at the grocery bags Bethany is carrying. "What are you making for dinner?"

DRIVING THE KID TO SCHOOL gives Jordy a reason to get up in the morning. Then he heads to the studio, where he spends several hours a day sorting through and testing cables and microphones, determining which work and which need to be thrown out and replaced.

Dave calls from San Francisco with depressing updates.

"You're not going to recognize the album. You won't even recognize your drumming with all the effects they're bastardizing it with. And the way they're manipulating his voice – it's unbelievable. They have him singing lyrics and melodies he never actually sang.

I'd say he's rolling over in his grave if he wasn't scattered across the Pacific Ocean. I was in the band, you'd think my opinion would count for something, but no, everyone just buys into the grieving widow."

Then Jordy picks up his nephew from school, or drives him to a friend's house. He passively scolds him when he comes home drunk, and he gives him advice on dating girls, slipping him an extra twenty so he can take his date somewhere nicer than the mall food court. He even trusts the kid enough to watch the baby one evening so he and Bethany can go out to dinner.

"You know, I had forgotten about you." His demeanor toward Bethany has softened since Michael's visit. "For years I thought I was doomed by your memory. Every day something reminded me of you. Then eventually I'd be lying in bed at night and realize I hadn't thought about you that day yet. Then I'd go a few days without thinking about you. Then weeks. Finally I just stopped. Completely."

"It was hard to forget you, too," she says. Probably harder, because Jordy had become a minor celebrity. She'd secretly bought all his band's albums. Then she had to buy them again after her husband discovered the first collection and threw it out.

Like Michael, Bethany finds it astounding that Jordy can't move on. Jordy was dumped by Michael about the same time she began rejecting his attempts to win her back; she remembers his dual heartache vividly. He quickly met Bradley and Dave and seemed to rebound fine. She never saw them perform, but he told her all about their first shows in the American Legion, friends' living rooms, and clubs with ten people in attendance. He was never more comfortable than when he was behind a drum set, although talking with Bethany was a close second. He could tell her everything.

For example:

Three different girls all openly "liked" Jordy. As a twenty-year-old with the maturity of a sixteen-year-old, this was as big a crisis as it was the coolest thing ever.

— Who do I ask out? Whose heart will I break? How do I handle this without making some enemies?

And so he sought the advice of his good friend, his best friend, really.

I'm sorry but I have to do it again. I will miss you, but your friendship is not worth the strain on my engagement. I wish you the best, and will pray for you always. Please don't call me. — Bethany

A note?! The first time, she'd told him over the phone. Now he doesn't even get the chance to plead his case. Jordy wept. Surely no one in the history of the world had ever felt pain the way he was hurting now.

Of the three girls, whatsername was the most immediately available. Twenty years of virginity gone in two minutes.

This was Jordy pointing his middle finger at God. Most of his friends treated sex as a recreational activity, like billiards, but until recently Jordy had been a regular churchgoer, and he considered sex a sacred experience, both physically and spiritually. Even feeling up Bethany initially terrified him. But it's human nature to rebel, and one can't rebel against God without believing He exists. He cast his reservations aside and, out of anger, his relationship with whatsername was born.

He broke it off with her between the band's first and second tours. His intention to be on the road for most of the foreseeable future rendered a steady girlfriend unnecessary. Though initially crushed, whatser-name accepted Jordy's lifestyle.

But, as a human male, Jordy was weak. Between tours, he accepted her invitations to bed. On her wall were posters of the band, and she gushed about how cool it was to be sleeping with a rock star. She begged him to marry her. He declined, but still they got together, three or four hookups a year whenever he happened to be home, until a few weeks after his most recent visit, when she called to tell him she was pregnant. He didn't believe her. Nor did he believe her when she said she'd had the baby. He moved back home after Bradley's death, and again she demanded that he marry her, or she'd kill herself, too. He called her bluff, kind of. She faked a suicide attempt, but faked it badly, so badly that she died. Hence the baby in Jordy's care.

He brought the baby home, more afraid than he'd ever been. Bethany re-entered his life the same day, like a guardian angel.

"Why wouldn't you marry her?" Bethany asks.

"I hated myself when I was with her. And I *really* hated myself after I was with her. No self-discipline, no self-esteem. Like I was cheating on something. And then we'd leave for tour and I'd barely give her a second thought until we got home and she'd call me again. There was nothing there. Not even a relationship to speak of. She wasn't the one. When you know, you know."

"I understand," Bethany says, patting his hand. "You really never loved her?"

"Pretty sure no," he says. "Pretty sure I've never loved anyone." He looks at Bethany. "Well..."

"I know."

Bethany is thrilled that Jordy's willingness to open up to her has returned. He treats her like a diary, the way he used to. She tries to convince him that he's not entirely to blame for whatsername's death. She lets him cry for the loss of Bradley. And he's scared of raising a baby. Bethany shows him how to feed and hold him, and she guides his attempts at changing diapers, offering instruction while stifling laughter at his ineptitude.

Said baby wakes up across the house, wailing.

"Aw, little guy is angry," Bethany says.

"Hasn't been changed in a while," Jordy says. "I got it."

"You sure?"

"I changed one yesterday," he boasts. "Didn't even gag."

Bethany smiles at him proudly. She reaches to caress his arm as he gets up. He's just out of reach.

"SOUNDS LIKE we're going to make some money," Jordy says.

Defeated, Dave tells of the label's plans to exploit Bradley's death, calling it an intentional suicide by the long-suffering artist, the key element in the marketing plan for the album.

"Probably a lot of money," Dave says. "And we'll be forever branded sellouts."

Now that he no longer has an album to fight for, Dave's plan is to grow their recording studio and start a new band. Jordy reminds Bethany and Dave that they met once upon a time at an MxPx concert, and they pretend to remember. Dave is shocked that the baby in this woman's arms is actually Jordy's, which puts a damper on things. But his plans are largely dependent on Jordy, so they'll make it work. Neither of them knows how to do anything else.

The former bandmates had gone to the grocer down the street, and now Jordy has four steaks searing on the stove, frozen French fries in the oven, and mixed vegetables boiling. And he set the table before Bethany even got wind of the dinner preparations.

Although the table is set for four, Jordy isn't positive his nephew is home until he walks down the stairs and into the kitchen to investigate the scents taking over the house.

"You remember Dave, right?" Jordy says. The nephew smiles and shyly looks at his shoes; his uncle is one thing, but Dave is a celebrity. He can't wait to brag about this to his friends. "Dave's staying for dinner."

"You're grilling steaks!" The nephew snaps out of it. "Sweet!" He skips out of the kitchen and kneels down to tickle the baby seated on Bethany's lap. Jordy savors the scene. Tomorrow he is taking his nephew home; the kid's mother wants him back.

Dave watches, too, and says, "Nice little family you've put together for yourself."

"It is," Jordy agrees.

After Dave leaves, Jordy sits Bethany on the couch with a magazine while he cleans up the kitchen. Later, he gives the baby a bottle, changes his diaper, and rocks him to sleep. Bethany looks on at first, but he has it under control.

THE DOOR TO BETHANY'S ROOM is ajar. Inside, she is changing for bed. Jordy can't help but peep; during the day, she dresses conservatively, without a hint of cleavage. She turns around and they make eye contact. He freezes, panics, and expects a scolding, but she doesn't say anything. Seconds pass before he averts his eyes and runs upstairs.

Lying in bed with his hand in his pants, he clings to the image. It's been ten years, and she's given birth, but she looks better than ever. He hears footsteps in the hall, then light knocking. The door opens and he recognizes Bethany's silhouette latching the door behind her. She lifts the covers and lies down, pulling Jordy's arm around her. She sighs; they spoon. Hard-on pressed against her ass, Jordy's heart races while Bethany sleeps soundly.

IN THE MORNING they have a leisurely family breakfast before Jordy's nephew finishes packing his belongings and carries them to the car.

"Time to give back the kid," Jordy says to Bethany. "Do you want to come?"

"I'll stay here. You have a nice time with your sister."

"Okay, too bad. I'm taking the little one, too, so he can get to know his auntie."

"Are you sure you can handle that?"

Jordy hasn't taken the baby anywhere since he first brought him home.

"Shouldn't be a problem."

"Good for you," she says, smiling sadly, proud of him. "And good luck."

The kid is already in the car, but Bethany kisses the baby, hugs Jordy, and stands outside the front door to wave goodbye.

Other than incidental contact passing the baby back and forth, Jordy and Bethany hadn't touched each other before last night. The softness of this hug lingers with Jordy.

After reuniting the kid and his mother, he stays only a short while, anxious for another shot at Bethany's arms.

"We're back!" Jordy calls as he carries the baby through the door. "And still in one piece, both of us!"

He doesn't hear anything. On the coffee table is a folded piece of paper.

— No, no, no, not again, please God, no, not again, please, please God, no, no, no.

He carries the baby with him to search the house. Her bed is perfectly made, her drawers empty, her shampoo missing from the shower. He concedes defeat, puts the baby on the floor, and takes the note.

Going back to my family. It was good to see you again. I love you, and will pray for you always. Thanks for everything. — Bethany

He reads it a hundred times before he folds it up and puts it in his pocket. *I love you*, she wrote. He chokes up; swallowing doesn't do any good.

"It's quiet," he says, sitting down on the floor. The baby bats a jingle toy. "Your cousin is gone." The baby waves his hand again, misses this time, briefly whines in frustration, then smacks it hard. "And mama's not coming back."

The baby puts his hands on the floor. Leaning forward, he pushes himself onto his knees and topples face-first into Jordy's lap. Frightened, he begins to cry.

DON'T MOVE

HE SHOUTS, "DON'T MOVE," and she freezes. Wide-eyed, she stares at him and dares to take a step. "Stop!" he yells. "Don't move an inch!" She's surrounded by peril, and he is the only other person here. Her bare feet remain firmly planted. He looks at the floor and at his *own* bare feet before taking *his* first step, a calculated move, carefully plotting his course. One step at a time, putting pressure only on the balls and toes, determined not to get cut, though, of course, he is of secondary importance.

"You're not in trouble; just *don't move*," he reiterates. Her body language threatens to disobey him. "Don't!" he shouts, this time the loudest yet, almost angry that she doesn't trust him. Finally he reaches her. She is shaking. His hands clasp on to her sides, and he picks her up by the armpits. She continues to shake but can't resist the feeling of comfort. He retraces his steps for both of them, harder this time, making it to safety.

"You're safe," he says, exhaling, reuniting her with the ground. Tears pour from the corners of her eyes. "You're okay now," he assures her.

"Don't yell at me!" his four-year-old shrieks, and runs away.

Sighing, he turns to get a broom and dustpan but steps on a shard of glass from the broken jar she had dropped.

DROP DOWN

WE'D BEEN UP IN THAT TREE FOREVER, it seemed, me and Janey. Thank God that girl came along. Otherwise, who knows how much longer we would've been trapped. Those fuckers weren't giving us a chance, that's for sure. There wasn't anything to do but sit and wait it out.

This was the most intimate we'd been. Together almost two weeks, but all that time, while walking around during the day or even setting up camp for the night, we could always be reasonably sure it was safe to go behind a tree and squat. We could even get a good ten or twenty yards away from each other for more privacy and still feel safe. Not up in that tree, though. We were comfortable enough that we didn't feel like we were going to fall at any second, but it wasn't like there was any-where else to go.

For me it was no big deal. I barely had to pull down for number one. And Janey would look down, or away, averting her eyes. And then I could just let it fly. Right on those fuckers' heads. Right into those fuckers' mouths. It was almost funny. Even Janey smiled.

For her it was a bigger deal. She had to pull down most of the way, and then girls have to squat, at least part way, and aiming was problematic.

"Should I just go in my pants?" she asked. She was uncomfortable not only because I might see, but because the crowd below would be watching. They didn't have the decency to shut their eyes.

Anyway, that's how it came up. We didn't know how long we were going to be up there, but we had a feeling it would be a while. And she was the first one to think about it. I told her she shouldn't. It was unhygienic, she might get an infection, it was kind of disgusting, it would smell, and she would be uncomfortable sitting there in wet shorts and underwear. It was up to her, of course, and she eventually agreed.

She stood up and, with one hand, grabbed hold of a branch above her. Balance was key. If we fell, then forget about it. Then she undid the button on her shorts with the free hand. She pushed them as far down as she could while still holding onto the branch, and then shimmied them the rest of the way to her ankles. With one arm wrapped around the trunk of the tree, I held on to her free hand so she could lean back slightly and take her own turn at pissing on those fuckers' heads. I tried not to look. I really didn't mean to, but I saw a little. I didn't tell her I did, though, and she didn't ask. Her aim was all right. She got a little bit on the branch we'd been sitting on, but not much. Not so much that we wouldn't sit back down.

"That went pretty well," I said, after we were re-situated on the branches. "No big deal, right."

"Right," she said, but her face was beet-red and stayed that way for a few minutes.

If there'd just been one down there, I could have taken it. I could have jumped on it and knocked it over. I could have kicked the hell out of its head, killing it senseless. Then hopefully Janey would have been able to drop down, no problem, and get a good distance away. And I could have run and caught up to her, and that would've been it.

But I'd never killed one before. That was unusual. I was lucky. I'd seen others kill them, but not me. They were monster-like enough, though, that I thought I would be able to without freaking out.

Janey had killed one, sort of. In the beginning, before we even met, she'd kicked one down the stairs and bashed its head open on the doorstop. I had to pull that story out of her; she didn't want to talk about it. I thought it must've been someone she was related to, like her brother, or mother, or father. Boyfriend? I didn't think she was old enough to have been married. Maybe. If she had been married, she would've gotten married pretty young.

"You can talk about it if you want," I said. "I'm a good listener."

She shook her head. "I'll never want to talk about it."

But there wasn't just one of them down there. There were ten. And they were persistent. There wasn't anywhere for us to go.

I couldn't believe what I was seeing. The girl was the first normal we'd seen since we climbed up there. We hadn't been talking much, me and Janey. She didn't say much to begin with. We weren't mad at each other, or anything, but now there really wasn't a whole lot to say. We were pretty cozy. I was leaning against the trunk, and she was leaning against me. We could practically hear each other's heartbeats and each other's stomachs growling.

I saw the girl first. Our tree was at the edge of a clearing, and the girl was in the middle of it. And it was a good-sized clearing, too, like a football field, only bigger. Maybe a couple of football fields. I nudged Janey and pointed out the girl.

And then one of the fuckers – not one of ours, but a different one – was walking toward her. And she didn't even notice. Like she didn't care, or maybe didn't realize.

In the girl's defense, some of them didn't look as bad as others. Some of them, especially the new ones, you had to look twice to know whether or not to avoid them. It wouldn't be hard to mistake one of them for a normal dude if it were dark, if you were tired or high, or if you lost your glasses.

I was worried about that last one. I had contacts in, and I had two spare sets in my backpack, and
I even had contact solution. That had been my biggest
concern when I realized I was going on the lam. The
contacts were in my backpack, and I kept my glasses in
one of the side pockets of my cargo shorts. Those were
more important. The contacts were way more comfortable, but they were disposables and weren't going
to last forever, even if I did.

Janey said she had perfect vision, so she didn't
have that to worry about. She was lucky. I was prepared to guard my glasses with my life. Except that
would defeat the purpose. I was already planning on
finding some way to strap the glasses around my head
so I wouldn't lose them during action. If those fuckers
ever let us down.

I don't know what I had been thinking with
those cargo shorts. It was already starting to get cold
at night. Once we were down – if – finding a pair of
long pants was going to be a priority. For Janey, too.
Her shorts were shorter than mine. She started shiver-
ing before the sun was even all the way down. I did
what I could to help keep her warm, but I couldn't do
much. I rubbed my bare legs against hers.

"Does that help at all?" I asked.

"I don't know," she said, and actually smiled.
"But it feels nice." Her face turned beet-red again.
Strange times to be a prude.

Going up in the tree was a bad idea. That's

obvious now. We were just so tired, though. There was an attack, and I thought I had lost Janey. Then I saw her running around the corner, pointing in one direction, so I went that way, too. And we couldn't stop. Those fuckers were relentless. Every time we thought we had lost them and took a moment to try to catch our breaths, they showed up again within a minute or two. We ran for hours. Finally, we were leaning against the tree and hadn't seen one of them for a few minutes. And we thought if we went up into the tree, out of their general field of vision, we could rest up a little longer, massage our hamstrings or whatever, and then get going. They never seemed to look up, not unless there was a reason to. We would just have to be quiet. No big deal.

It might've worked if we were faster. Janey got up, no problem, but I was still dangling when one of those fuckers came through a clearing and saw my legs for a split-second. It started pawing at the tree like an idiot. Then another one showed up, and another, and finally ten. They didn't leave, and they didn't lose focus. They just stared at us, waiting. There had been ten of them, surrounding us, the whole time.

What I should've done was hop down and run off immediately. That first one would've followed me and left Janey to rest up in the tree, undetected. And after a bit, she would have been able to get down and run off herself. But if that had happened, I might not have found her again. I thought if we ever got down, I was going to make Janey promise, no more trees, ever.

I'd been in a group for a couple weeks before running into Janey. It was a big group. People kept getting picked off. We'd lose one or two every other day or so, but we'd pick up stragglers along the way and replace them. People really bought into the whole safety-in-numbers thing. Then we got ambushed, and I lost everyone.

Janey had actually hidden out in her house for a while. That must've been great. She got forced out eventually. She hooked up with a couple of people, but they both got nabbed. After she ran into me, we were together most of the day before I asked what her name was.

"So, do you want to know mine, then?" I asked next.

She shook her head. "Not really."

"Why not?"

"Because," she said. "Maybe it won't hurt as much when I lose you."

I didn't know how we were going to get down, but we needed to, or we were going to starve. What little water we had was already gone. What little food we had was already gone. Finding food hadn't been an issue when we were on the ground, but we were always on the move and hadn't stocked up, just whatever fit in my backpack. I didn't think it would be hard to find something once we were down.

There were leaves on the tree. I ate some

leaves. They were okay. Janey ate some leaves, too. But it was September. There weren't going to be leaves on the trees forever, and who knows what they would do to our digestion.

I didn't mind knowing I was going to die, but I didn't want to know I was dying. I didn't want to starve to death in a few days, but the other option - jumping down from the tree - guaranteed pain and suffering. I didn't want pain and suffering.

I had my eye on this rock. I figured I could dive onto it. I didn't want to be conscious after I landed, but if I landed head first on the rock I might die on impact. Or at least I might be knocked unconscious and not know that I was dying until later, after I was already dead. And while they were busy with me, maybe Janey could get down and run away. I didn't say it out loud, but that was all preferable to starving. As long as my head didn't miss the rock. I wondered if Janey had given it any thought.

And then that stupid girl. She was our savior. Maybe I should've tried to warn her. She practically walked right up to that fucker, so nonchalantly that I thought maybe it was a normal dude after all. We couldn't actually tell from that distance, even with Janey's twenty-twenty vision and my contacts in. But it grabbed at her. She might've been burnt out before, but now she screamed. She screamed loud, but there was no way she was getting away from it. And it took its time on her, too, going to town on her mid-section. And all the while, she kept on screaming.

That got the attention of our fuckers below. Like they instantly forgot about us. Probably did, they were so stupid. One-track minds. They all started rushing best they could toward the commotion, like a bunch of morons. Janey and I watched the carnage, hardly believing our good luck. Eventually the girl stopped screaming, and it was just a pile of fuckers on top of each other, like pigs at a trough.

I nudged Janey and gestured that it was time to go. Before we could even make a move, though, there was more screaming. It was a couple of normals on the far side of the clearing. Probably the girl's friends. They turned around and ran in the opposite direction. They had a good head start, but the pile of fuckers chased after them, anyway, except for a couple that stayed behind to finish up the girl.

It was too bad about her, but it was good for Janey and me. We were finally getting out of that tree.

SPIDERS

SOMETIMES, AFTER I LEAVE MY GIRLFRIEND'S to drive home at night, there's a spider on my windshield. It always sort of freaks me out, because I can never tell right away whether it's inside the car or out. I'm not afraid of spiders; I just don't like them.

So far, though – thanks to my habit of making sure the windows are closed, all the way, no matter what, because of that one time they weren't, it down-poured, and I had to drive home sitting in a puddle – they've always been outside. Then all I have to do is turn the wipers on to sweep the spider off, or, better yet, fatally mangle it. After that, except for the remains of spider guts and a leg or two, I can forget about it.

But tonight, for the first time ever, this spider was out of reach of the wiper blades. I went to spray it off with windshield washer fluid, but the tank was dry.

No big deal, I reassured myself. Once I start moving, the spider will blow away.

But my girlfriend lives in this residential neigh-borhood where the speed limit is 25 and there are stop signs every two hundred feet. I never see them, but there is always a cop whenever I do something stupid, like go 55 in a 25, so I stayed slow. Ready to leave the tract and stopped at a stop sign under the glow of a street light, I saw that, other than maybe an inch and a half, the spider hadn't moved.

I guess I wasn't surprised but it was still a bummer. In a few more turns, I'd be on a 55, and if the spider was still on the windshield by the time I got there, it wouldn't be for long.

Each time I drove under a street light, I searched the windshield for the spider. It was crouched down in a defensive position, holding on for dear life. I turned onto the 55 and floored it. I went under a green light and the glow showed it was still there.

I'm not afraid of spiders, I swear, but when I see one crawling across my floor I involuntarily bolt for a clump of tissues to grab it with, and sprint to the toilet to flush it down. I'd rather not do this, but it's their own dumb fault for coming into the house in the first place. If they hadn't done what they're not supposed to do, they'd still be alive. I explain this to them on our trips to the toilet, as if to teach them a lesson, even though none of them ever get a second chance to do the right thing.

The light was green, and I took the next left turn faster than usual, hoping that the spider would lose its balance and fly off. It didn't. It might've moved a half an inch or so, but even that I wasn't sure of. I didn't think it was dead, but maybe it had frozen stiff in the chilly high winds.

My best friend is deathly afraid of spiders. It's funny because he's a guy-guy. We listen to punk rock and have tried to pick up girls together, and he's a way better baseball player than me. When he sees a spider, though, he screams like a ten-year-old girl.

"Oh my God, there's this huge spider over there," he would say, backing away. If I took his descriptions literally, the spider on my windshield would be the size of one of those tarantulas in the beginning of *Raiders of the Lost Ark*.

When we were kids, his basement was the worst for spiders. All the time we'd be down there looking at baseball cards and inevitably he'd see one and flip out. He had pinpoint accuracy with a baseball, but his aim was garbage while chucking shoes at a spider twenty feet away. I always had to step up to save the day. I'm not afraid of spiders, but I don't like killing them. I don't know why they can't just stay outside. It wasn't enough, though, that the spider on my windshield was outside. Its mistake was not keeping its distance and staying out of sight.

In my younger years I used to kill spiders outside with a hose. I liked playing with the hose, as children do, and I volunteered whenever possible to water the flowers. Sometimes a spider web had formed between the siding of the house and the bushes. Then I liked to put the hose on the jet setting, full blast, and power wash it out of there. If there was a spider on the web, I had something to aim for. Kids can be cruel.

With all the attention I was giving the spider,

it was a testament to my superb driving skills that I stayed on the road. I was so afraid I would miss the moment it would finally fly off. But it hadn't even changed positions, like it was suction-cupped to the glass.

With every turn, I thought we might slow down enough for it to be able to get up and move around. Maybe it would walk into the line of windshield wiper fire. But at this point, wipers seemed like cheating. I wanted it whisked away, like Dorothy, and her little dog, too.

We got on the expressway where the speed limit was 65. That means you can go 75. It seemed like forever went by before my little putt-putt hatchback got up that fast. I hit 70. The spider was still there. There were never any cops on that road, so I sped up to 80, and then touched 85. For anyone riding on top of the car, this was hurricane-like wind. And it was still there! In half a mile, the speed limit decreased from 65 to 55, so I let off the gas some. This spider was like an alien life form. I was pretty sure *I* would've blown off after two seconds.

One time I had these itchy little bumps on one side of my stomach. Somebody told me it might be shingles. Somebody else thought they were spider bites, and that a spider trapped in my bed had bit me a few times. Spiders would have been easiest to deal with because we could just wash the sheets and that would be it. The thought of sleeping with a spider freaked me out, though, so, even though I'd never heard of it before, I rooted for shingles. Then I went to an actual doctor, who granted my wish. He gave me some creams, but it was still the most discomfort I'd ever felt in my life.

I wondered if the spider on my windshield could be a symbol for something. Maybe, I thought, I could use it as an example of something that never gives up. I could use it as a metaphor to motivate my kids or students or someone, an alternate version of the tortoise and the hare.

I was probably twelve or thirteen when my dad, my younger sister, and I were driving back from my grandparents' in Pennsylvania with a bunch of boxes that had been stored in a basement. It was after dark when my sister, sitting alone in the backseat, let out a blood-curdling scream. It scared my dad and me half to death. While my dad pulled over to the side of the thruway, I looked back. Judging from her scream, sitting next to her *should* have been a serial killer with a long, pale face, wearing a trench coat, and holding a bloody knife.

"I saw a spider," she explained. There was no serial killer, but I thought I saw the silhouette of a spider on the back window.

My dad was a little upset, because her scream had almost driven us off the road and killed us all. My sister got out of the car and whimpered by the side of the road while my dad and I searched the car for the spider. We didn't find anything. We figured it crawled out of the car while the doors were open, if it did in fact exist. My dad talked me into taking the backseat and let my sister sit in the front. I wasn't afraid, but it sure was easier to relax before I thought there could be a spider in the car.

Now I'm the driver, and it's time to exit the expressway. We hit a couple more green lights and the spider had to stay put. I had hit all green lights, and I should've appreciated shooting the moon more, but I was too distracted by the spider's will to live. I wondered if it had ever traveled this far before. I suddenly felt bad taking it from its friends and families. It would probably never have the chance to tell them about its incredible journey, although if it were smart, it would realize I'd probably be going back to my girlfriend's the next day. It could hitch a ride easily enough. Except that I planned on killing it as soon as I got out of the car. Because I don't like spiders.

I was never one of those kids that pulled the wings off of flies, or the legs off of spiders. I never burned ants with a magnifying glass. I was looking forward to crushing this spider, though. I was going to crush it good.

We were in the city, where the speed limits were lower and traffic was heavier. My next turn was a right turn, but the light was red and there were cars in front of me, giving me no chance to go through without stopping. I slowed way down, hoping that the light would change, but at last we came to a standstill. And the spider budged.

The spider's legs stretched out, and it started

moving, as if nothing had happened. It didn't even seem sore from crouching down for so long. It must have been disoriented, though, because instead of going up top and out of harm's way, it went down, into the middle of the windshield, where it was wiper territory. If I'd wanted, I could have finally wiped it off the windshield and erased it from existence, as if I were God.

The light changed. I made my turn, and the spider crouched down again, freezing into position right in the middle of my windshield. The kill zone. I didn't have any washer fluid, though, nor did it look like it was going to rain soon, and I don't like having bits of spider on my windshield.

The Who have a song about a spider. The singer describes the spider crawling up the wall and moving about the room. He thinks maybe the spider is just as scared as he is. Then, when it's not moving, "Perhaps he's dead, I'll just make sure." The spider's name was Boris. He sure came to a messy end. I bet the song is really about drugs.

Two more quick turns, and I pulled into the driveway. For only the second time since leaving my girlfriend's, we came to a complete stop. The spider stretched out again and started crawling, only this time it crawled up.

I got out of the car and found the spider up top. It was small. It looked a lot smaller outside than it had from inside. I made a fist and prepared to smash it. But I didn't want spider guts on my hand, even if it were only for a few seconds before I could get to a sink.

The spider scurried across the length of the car toward the back. I got ready to flick it off and let it go sailing into the dark, cold grass, soaking with dew. It started crawling down the back window and my feet shuffled to follow alongside.

What a stupid, helpless creature.

I'm inside now, giving it a head start. If it's still around in the morning, I'll kill it then.

END

ACKNOWLEDGMENTS

Several of these stories have been published previously: "Tadpoles" in *Steam Ticket*; "The Dog's Fault" in *Midnight Special*; "Sweet Gum Tree" in *Bodega Magazine*; "Not Leaving Without My Boy" in *Tethered By Letters*; "Unearthing" in *Midwest Writers Guild Literary Journal*; "Befriending the Scum of the Earth" in *The Bombay Review*; and "Drop Down" in *Typehouse Literary Magazine*. Thank you to the editors of these publications for championing my work.

Frank Gordon deserves much of my gratitude for providing the cover art, as does Amber Heerdink for the photography.

Many thank yous go out to Tim Heerdink, Paul Britton, and Holly Jennings for being my primary readers and givers of feedback, for their encouragement and constructive criticism.

And, of course, thank you to Bird Brain Publishing for having enough confidence in me to add this collection to its list of titles.

Joshua Britton is a professional trombonist living in Evansville, Indiana, with his wife and two small children. *Tadpoles* is his first book.

www.joshua-britton.com

joshua_britton@yahoo.com

Twitter: @JP_Britton